LONGING FOR EVER AFTER

Sunset Bay Romance, Book Four

DEBRA CLOPTON

CHAPTER ONE

Jonah Sinclair walked down the streets of Sunset Bay, heading toward the long pier and the ice cream cone that was calling his name.

"Hey, Jonah, I hear you and your brothers are competing in the Sunset Bay Regatta." Hal, the owner of the Pier Ice Cream Shop, handed him his waffle cone of chocolate turtle ice cream.

Jonah took the cone and passed Hal his money. "Yeah, can you believe it? We haven't competed together in years. Not since Adam headed off to medical school and Tate took off to who knows where." He grinned. Tate's whereabouts had been a running joke ever since he managed to make a living out of his adventurous escapades and everyone always asked where he was. Half the time, the family couldn't keep his schedule straight.

Hal chuckled. "That's the truth. It will be good to see you all together out there again."

"Thanks, and thanks for this." Jonah lifted his cone in salute then headed toward the railing to watch the boats in the bay and the people fishing from the pier.

He enjoyed people-watching at the huge, long public pier. It was a fun place. Tourists who didn't have a boat came here and enjoyed the day. And families especially enjoyed time together here. Watching them, he realized that, probably soon, at least one of his siblings who had just married the loves of their lives would probably announce they were having a baby. He figured it would be Adam and Rosie, but Brad and Lulu might beat them. Erin had just gotten engaged to Nash, so he figured they had awhile yet. It was between Adam and Brad to be the first of the six Sinclairs to make their mother ecstatic. Not that either of them were planning a family just to make Maryetta and Leo—their parents—happy; they were both ready to go all-in on their futures.

He licked his cone and tried not to dwell on the fact that the right woman didn't seem to be in his future. He'd wanted a wife and kids far longer than any of his brothers or sisters, and yet it hadn't happened for him. And after too many disappointments, he'd grown weary of looking for her. Endless dates had ended with him feeling down, and constantly having to push himself to go on another date, only to realize pretty quickly that this one wasn't her either. It had just soured him on the whole dating scene and made him think maybe marriage wasn't in his future.

So, it had been awhile since he'd made himself ask someone out. He was just having to get used to the hole in his life and hoped that watching his siblings have what he wanted was enough for him.

Today, there seemed to be couples everywhere, reminding him that he was here alone and feeling dissatisfied. He had a good life, a great business and, most of the time, a positive attitude. But more and more, he was feeling really lonely.

A little girl with a big ice cream cone stopped a few feet in front of him. She was really cute, with curly dark hair and the face of a little angel.

She licked the ice cream then looked up at him with a big dazzling smile. "Hi, mister. I got a vanilla ice cream cone. What kind you got?"

He smiled back at her. "I've got chocolate turtle."

Her green eyes widened. "Turtle? They make turtle ice cream?"

He almost laughed but held it back at the alarm in her eyes. "No, it means chocolate ice cream with nuts and caramel inside."

Her brows dipped. "Oh. That's good. We shouldn't eat turtles. I love them and wouldn't want people to eat them."

"I agree," he said. She couldn't be more than five, maybe six. He wondered where her mother was. He looked around and saw a woman with long brown hair rushing their way.

"Polly, you were to stand right beside me until I

paid." Concern etched her pretty face as she reached the girl.

"I know. But I needed to talk to this man." She grinned up at Jonah and he looked from the child to her beautiful mother.

"Of course, you did, Polly." She looked from her child to Jonah. He felt a kick in his gut as gorgeous emerald eyes met his. "I hope she wasn't bothering you."

"N-no, not at all."

They stared at each other and a hundred questions flowed through his mind that he wanted to ask her. But he didn't.

"You have a boat." Polly tilted her head as she continued to stare up at him with her big emerald eyes, that definitely were a gift from her mother.

"Yes, I do. How did you know?"

"We saw you." Polly licked her ice cream.

"Yes, we did," her mother added. She dipped her spoon into the cup of pink ice cream she was holding. "We were walking along the docks earlier and saw you on your boat. Polly takes in everything."

"Sorry, I didn't see you." He must have had his head down because he would never have missed her passing by otherwise. He watched her take a bite of the ice cream before she answered him.

"You were busy getting the boat in order. And we were not that close to your boat, anyway. Polly said you looked like the caricature on the sign. You know, the one for the boat rental and storage company."

He laughed. "Good eye. I'm Jonah, of Jonah's Boat Rentals."

"I knew it was you." Polly beamed, ice cream surrounding her mouth.

"Is it really you?" the mother asked.

He found himself drawn to her. "Yeah. If you ever want to go out…I mean take her out on a boat, just let me know. It's what I do."

She looked suddenly uncomfortable. "Thanks, but I'd have to ask her daddy. Polly, we need to go. Have a nice evening." Then she took Polly's hand and stepped away.

Polly smiled, her mouth still circled with white melted ice cream. "It was nice meeting you. And maybe my daddy will let me go on the boat with you. I'll ask him. Bye."

"Sounds good," he managed as he watched them walk away, hand in hand. He realized he hadn't gotten the little girl's mother's name. Not that it mattered. She was married. And that was just the way his luck had been running these days. He hadn't felt a real spark of attraction in a while, and when he finally did, it was toward a beautiful, married woman.

He sighed. Maybe he needed to get back in the game, the endless dating game that seemed to always come up empty for him. The game he'd grown so weary of putting out the effort for. But he didn't go for married women; the fact that even after knowing she was married he still had this lingering attraction to her told him it was time.

He'd obviously been lonelier than he'd admitted.

As much as he dreaded the thought of more rejection and disappointment, he was going to cautiously get back in the dating waters. And then it would start: as word got out he was looking again, there would be the hounding of his mother and a host of local ladies coming after him with more of their endless, good-intentioned, plans to fix him up.

He tossed his melting ice cream in the trash and headed back toward the docks where his truck was parked. It seemed a man should be more excited about looking for love, or his very own happily-ever-after.

But love and ever-after hadn't been his friend. He could only hope this time his luck would change.

* * *

Summer Claremont walked away from the pier, holding her niece's hand. Why hadn't she told the handsome, gorgeous man that Polly wasn't hers? Of course, she knew why: she wasn't ready for a man to look at her the way he had looked at her. Jonah, he'd said, was his name; a nice name for someone who seemed like a very nice person.

Before she had even met him, when she and Polly were walking along the docks and Polly had pointed him out to her, she'd admired the look of him. Which was also something she hadn't thought she was ready for. She'd come a long way in the six months since she had been attacked. She still couldn't talk about it, still couldn't function like she once had. The fact that she had walked the pier in this small town had amazed her. And then again, that was the reason her brother had suggested she make the move with him and Polly. He wanted her to come along and be Polly's nanny while he took his new job here in Sunset Bay. And at first, she had said no, not being able to leave her career behind. But she was on a leave of absence for medical reasons that at this point were psychological reasons more than physical. She knew she wasn't going to be able to go back to work in the downtown Houston high-rise that she had once worked in. She didn't think she would ever be able to go inside a parking garage again. Not if she didn't want to completely flip out and have another episode.

Her brother had wanted to help her and his offer was exactly what she needed. They could help each other out through the tough times in both of their lives. Her poor brother had lost his wife tragically and was now trying to raise their child, who was struggling to find her way. She also needed Summer. So, she had agreed and here she was in this gorgeous, little beach town on the coast of Florida.

Sunset Bay—just the name alone filled her with thoughts of a quaint beach town. And she hadn't been disappointed when they arrived three days ago and moved into the house that movers had already unpacked. Everything had already been set in rooms and she'd just had to straighten it up a bit. Now they were settling in.

The day they had driven through town the first time, her heart had breathed a sigh of relief. Unlike Destin and Houston, there were no high-rises here. As if it had been forgotten or something when the big resorts had staked out their claims on beaches across Florida. It was lovely. Hope brimmed through her that maybe here she could recover, that maybe she could get over being afraid of the dark, of shadows. That maybe she could get over the fear and panic that assaulted her when someone approached her from behind.

Maybe here, spending time playing with sweet

Polly every day on the beach and wandering the streets, exploring the shops like the little muffin shop, Bake My Day, could help her and Polly. Each of them had their own inner demons to overcome…maybe here she could become almost the person she had once been. But that didn't include a man or dating. After what she'd been through, she wasn't sure when she would be able to let a man touch her, much less put his arms around her.

So why in the world had she felt such an attraction to the man on the pier? She had never even believed that she would feel attraction again. She was usually so leery it was excruciating. And she had never been one to be scared before. Now she had to fight not to look over her shoulder all the time. She analyzed her path to wherever she was going before she got out of her car in order to time it as to minimize the people around her. She had always been the one to take the lead; now, she shrank behind like a frightened puppy. She had always been the friend who drew others out, but now she was the person in need of drawing out. She had never been this person she was now until some creep had come along and decided to…change her life.

Needless to say, she was not at the place she needed to be right now. She was not healthy or well or over it. And she couldn't honestly say when that would be. But she was determined to find herself again. It was just going to take time. And that time did not include thoughts of a handsome, kind, gorgeous man with eyes that seemed to look into her soul.

What a thought. No, this Jonah was off-limits.

And sooner or later, he would find out that she wasn't married. So why hadn't she told him that Polly was her niece and her dad was her big brother? She wasn't going to analyze the reasons; it didn't matter anyway.

"Aunt Summer." Polly looked up at her as they reached the car. "He was really nice. And I think he liked you. He sure did smile at you."

"How old are you, anyway, little woman? These are things that shouldn't even be popping into your head."

"I'm five and I know when a nice man smiles at a lady that he likes her."

The look on Polly's face was priceless. The child was precocious and bright and exactly the personality to remind Summer of how she had once been and wanted to get back to being. "Well, you might be right about that, but it doesn't matter anyway. I think he likes you best. You're the one who went and found him. And speaking of that, little lady, don't run away from me again. I mean it. You always have to be cautious and we don't know this town yet. Plus, we were on a pier. You know that water's down there."

Polly just stopped and looked at her as if she had lost her mind. Her big green eyes and dark curly hair shook as she slung her head from side to side in a gesture that said Summer was hopeless. "I'm *five*. I'm not going to go jump off the pier into the water. I know that I could get hurt. And I knew where you were— you were right there at the ice cream place, so I wasn't lost. I just saw him, and I knew we had seen him on the pier so I just went to say hello. And he looked lonely sitting up there, eating his ice cream cone by himself."

Oh, my goodness. "Polly, I know that you think that you're old enough to do things without any worry.

But, believe me, you're five and no, you're not able to go talk to random people you decide you want to talk to. Especially if I'm not near you. And I was having to pay for the ice cream."

Something in her tone must have told Polly that she was serious. The child looked down at the ground and looked back up at her with remorse. "Yes, Aunt Summer. I promised Daddy that I would not cause you trouble. And I don't want to. It's just I get a little excited sometimes and my feet just go where they want to go. So, I'll try hard not to do that again. Okay?"

Summer laughed, so thankful for this precocious child who was helping ground her. She scooped Polly into a big hug. Oh, how much she needed this. "Do you know how much I love you?"

Polly put her arms around Summer. "To the moon and back and a whole bunch of times around and then again. I love you the same."

"Two peas in a pod, aren't we?" Summer said with a chuckle and released her.

"Yes, we are," Polly mimicked in her child's voice. "Two peas in a pod."

CHAPTER TWO

On his way back from the dock, Jonah detoured by the firehouse. He decided to check in on his brother Brad, the fire chief. He was one of the ones who was making him rethink getting back to dating. First, his brother Adam married Rosie, then Brad married Lulu, and now, his sister Erin had accepted Nash's proposal of marriage and it had started Jonah wishing again for a wife and kids. He wanted to be settled and living his dream. There had to be someone out there for him. Maybe he had just given up too early.

It hadn't just been that he'd given up; he was busy building the other part of his dream, his boat rental company. It had gotten really busy and the boat storage, too, as more and more people started coming to the area and bringing their boats with them. Business was booming and the bank account was growing. But was he ever going to have anyone to share it with?

Brad stood outside the firehouse, talking to a guy he didn't recognize. The man was dark-headed, lean and muscular. He was fit and wore a Sunset Bay Fire Department shirt. Jonah assumed this must be the new firefighter who Brad had told him was coming to town.

As Jonah approached, Brad grinned. "Hey, brother, glad you dropped by. I want to introduce you to Hunter Claremont. He just moved in—what, three days ago?"

Hunter nodded at the three days ago that Brad had said and held out his hand to Jonah. "Nice to meet you. Yeah, I moved in with my daughter. We're getting settled. I don't start until tomorrow but thought I'd stop by to talk to your brother and get a feel for the place."

Jonah put his hands on his hips after they'd shaken hands. "Glad to meet you. I have the boat rental down at the docks. You ever want to take a boat out, if you don't have your own, all you have to do is come see me and I'll lend you one. No charge for the police or firemen."

Hunter looked thoughtful as he crossed his arms. "I might do that. I had a boat but…well, I don't anymore. I'll let you know if I want to get out on the water. I might see about getting my daughter out there. She used to love it."

Brad and Jonah both grinned.

Jonah spoke first. "Kids love boats. Where did you move here from?"

"Destin. Just needed a change of scenery. And I've heard a lot of good things about the town and just thought this was a good fit for me and my daughter. And my sister. She's with us, too. She's going to be like the nanny. She's here from Houston."

Jonah wondered where Hunter's wife was but understood there were a lot of reasons he might not have a wife. "Well, we're glad you're here."

Brad studied him. "Got something on your mind?"

"It can wait."

Hunter held a hand up. "I was just about to leave, so if it's something personal, don't worry, I'm on my way. I've got to get back to the house for supper anyway."

"I don't want to run you off. Nothing I've got is that important."

Hunter shook his head. "I need to go anyway. I've got a couple of important people waiting for me at home. I don't want to keep them waiting so I'll say good-bye. I'll see you tomorrow bright and early, Brad. Thanks again for this opportunity."

"Thank you for accepting the job. You are truly needed," Brad said.

They watched Hunter walk to where his truck was parked. He climbed into the white truck and waved as he pulled away from the curb.

"Seems like a nice guy."

Brad nodded. "Yeah, I think he'll be a good addition. So, what's on your mind? I can tell something's ticking up there behind those eyes of yours."

"For one, don't tell Erin I told you, because I'm sure they're going to spring it on everybody, but I went by to check on Erin, and Nash was there."

"No kidding?"

"Yeah. Here we thought he had skipped out on her but he came back and asked her to marry him."

"All right, Nash Bond."

"Yeah, so looks like we're going to have another wedding."

"That's seriously great."

Jonah laughed. "Seriously. I was worried about her, you know. She looked really upset, even though she wasn't saying a whole lot at Mom and Dad's earlier. I wanted to make sure she was okay. I thought I was going to have to fly to New York and meet up with the guy. Which I didn't want to do, because I like him. That was half the problem."

"Yeah, but I figured there was more to the story than him just leaving. Least, I hoped so. I'm glad he's back and I'm really happy. I'm sure we'll be hearing something soon. I wouldn't doubt if Lulu hears about it before I do, or I'm supposed to. I'm going to pretend this conversation never happened. I don't want to mess up her fun if she gets a call and then comes to spring it on me."

Jonah laughed. "I understand. But I needed to talk to you." He sighed. "I want to start dating again."

Brad grinned. "It's about time."

"I know, but you know how old it gets dating and never finding the right one. Seemed like there for the longest time, I was just hitting one bad date after the other. And I don't want to sound ungrateful. I mean, I dated a lot of nice women, but I wasn't looking for simply a nice woman—I was looking for the *right* woman. I just took this hiatus and then kind of settled into this ho-hum me and my ice cream cone in the evenings kind of routine. Kind of ridiculous, huh?"

Brad laughed and grinned real wide. "I've been wondering when you were going to come around and back to life. I thought you were going to end up being the old man bachelor of the family. You are the one I thought would be the first to get married out of all of us. It was a little bit confusing."

"Sorry I confused you." Jonah gave his brother a grin.

"I'll live. Since you're going to go for it now, do you have anybody in mind?" Brad started walking back into the firehouse and Jonah followed him. A group of the firemen were gathered in the kitchen but they bypassed it and went into Brad's office, which was in the front of the station. He had a window that overlooked the street and the dog park across the way. And across the dog park was the other side of town where Lulu's new pet daycare was.

Jonah still couldn't get over how they had met and what brought them together. Maybe something like that might happen to him. Some woman might decide that he was just what she was looking for and magic would happen. *In his dreams.*

He sat down in the seat across from Brad's desk. "I don't have anybody in mind." He raked a hand through his hair, reminding himself he needed a haircut. But he wasn't worried about that right now. He let his hand drop to the desk and he drummed his fingertips on the solid oak surface.

"Come on, spit it out. What is up?"

He groaned. "Okay, here it is. I saw a woman today, and for the first time in forever, she stirred my interest and spurred me into rethinking about dating again. Thing is, she's married and it's bothering the fire out of me that I was attracted to a married lady. She had her little girl with her. That's another reason I'm jumping back into the dating pool—because obviously, I need some female companionship."

Brad's brow creased. "Did you see a ring on her finger?"

Jonah thought about it for a minute. "Man, I have been out of it for so long, I didn't even think to look at her finger. I don't have a clue whether she had a ring on or not. But she mentioned her husband."

"Do you think she was a local or a tourist?"

"I think she's local, maybe new to town. I got that impression, anyway. But we met at the pier and you know how many tourists come to the pier. They were having ice cream, too. Little girl was cute, with dark curly hair. The woman was gorgeous, with straight dark hair. You know I'm not into married women and so it's bothering me. Besides, I'm never going to have kids if I don't find myself a wife. And I'm getting a little bored just having my ice cream cone all by my lonesome self."

Brad laughed. "You've got it made. You've got that great business. You have access to all these boats you could go play on the water and hang out in. You can make your own schedule and work when you want, you're rolling in the dough so deep. But you don't—you just keep on working." He grinned, loving to tease him about being rich and living the easy life.

Jonah laughed. "I'm rolling in about as much as you are." He had a great business with a lot of debt, but it was doing well and he wasn't hurting. But he wasn't rolling in the dough and Brad knew that. He just loved to tease.

Brad's grin mellowed. "You're still the catch of Sunset Bay."

"Yeah, right. But seriously, I guess, if you think of anybody, let me know. I'm going to start keeping my eyes open."

And he was going to put the dark-haired beauty out of his thoughts.

* * *

On Wednesday, Jonah was working on one of his boats. Though he had help whose job this was to do, he still helped out when they needed him to. Lately, because they were so busy, he stayed busy too. Especially now, in late August, as people were getting in the last of their vacations before school started. Boat rentals were at a high, so once the boats were brought in from the day, they had to all be washed and ready for tomorrow.

He was washing down the deck of one when he looked across the marina and saw her.

She sat at the far corner of the concrete walk along the docks and had her easel set up and was painting. From where she was sitting, he assumed she was painting a picture of the marina. Polly, her daughter, was nowhere in sight. Maybe the little girl was with her daddy. Or maybe she was in daycare. He had the strongest urge to go over and ask her whether she was, indeed, married—or at least, like Brad had pointed out, see whether she wore a ring. Not checking out her ring finger had been a mistake. But he couldn't bring himself to go over and talk to her and check things out.

Sunset Bay was a small town. He would run into her again and he'd be sure to look at her ring finger. And if there was no ring, he would ask her point-blank whether she was married. It was ridiculous, this tug he felt toward her. He had just briefly talked to her that day at the pier, and yet he was still thinking about her.

He'd been thinking about who in town he should ask out on a date, too. There were a lot of single women and he also rented boats out to tourists all the time, too, so he had plenty of ladies to choose from. But he hadn't done it yet.

He turned his back to her, determined to wash the boat down and not do something he would regret. He wasn't at all the sort of guy who would daydream about someone else's wife. It really bothered him. Laying down the water hose, he grabbed the bucket of water and cleaner and moved to the exterior of the boat, where he wiped it down. It was a hot, sweaty business and took concentration to get all the salt spray off the sides of the boat. He was meticulous with his fleet. Maintaining them kept them looking great. *How old was she?* He knocked the thought out of his mind and concentrated harder on the side of the boat.

He was going to the firehouse at six for a welcome to the community dinner for the new fireman, Hunter, and his family. He'd have to finish this up and then shower and change so he wouldn't be late. Home for him wasn't that far; it was just the apartment above the large boating garage that spread out over a considerable amount of square footage. One day he planned to buy a home but until he had a wife, there was no reason for him to live anywhere else but above his business. He had an amazing view, with wide windows that overlooked the bay and the ocean beyond and a huge deck to enjoy also. It was a priceless view, basically, so why would he want to give that up? Finding places on the bay wasn't cheap. Besides, that helped him continue building a very nice nest egg for when he did marry.

It was for the future. A future he was beginning to wonder whether he was ever going to fulfill.

Finishing up the boat, he let himself glance over but she wasn't there anymore. She had packed up her easel and gone. A sense of relief and regret filled him. He was really messed up.

He headed up to his apartment to shower and changed into cargo shorts and a cotton shirt. Then he headed toward the firehouse. A lot of people were already there by the time he rounded the corner and crossed the street. He spotted Nash Bond and his sister Erin. His mom and dad were with them and beaming; they must have just learned that Nash and Erin were engaged.

His mom, Maryetta, was out to get all of her kids married. It wasn't that she was hounding them—not really, anyway—or trying to fix them up, thank goodness. But she had made her wishes known and had basically told them that they were old enough to get married and why were they hem-hawing around? She was ready for grandchildren. It made sense. His mother had six kids and none of them, until just six months ago, had married. And they were all approaching thirty or right over the age of thirty. He could see her frustrations. But until now, he hadn't been on board despite being the one everyone had assumed would marry first.

And he wasn't telling anyone other than Brad that he was starting to look again.

He spotted Lila Peabody, Mami Desmond, Birdie Carmichael, and Doreen Posey, the group of older ladies he had dubbed the town matchmakers. These four older ladies spent a few hours a week at his sister-in-law, Rosie's, bakery, Bake My Day, plotting and talking about who in town they could fix up next. Or who in town they could at least shove in the direction of dating in the hopes that they would have a wedding to go to. At least, he assumed that was their only incentive for trying to match singles up. It wasn't as if Sunset Bay was lacking married couples and kids; they had plenty of them. It was just this group of four seemed to enjoy the process. Plus, it gave them something to gossip about. He wasn't sure whether he had come across their radar yet, so he side-stepped them and went around another group of people talking in order to avoid getting in their line of sight.

He spotted Adam and Rosie and headed over toward them. "Hey, how's it going?"

"Jonah, hey yourself. Glad you made it." Adam grinned and held his hand out. They shook and Jonah gave his sister-in-law a hug.

"We're doing great." She smiled up at him. "How about you? It was a great day—I'm sure you had a wonderful time out on the water."

"It was a good day. Sun was out, sky was gorgeous, and, of course, the water was clear and calm. It was a little bit hot since the breeze was laying low today but we're in paradise and have to take the good with the bad." He grinned. "But the water sure was pretty, all glassy and calm like that. Adam, did old man Larson come in?"

"With a hook in his finger. Yep, and he was not happy about it. He's been fishing so many years that he didn't think he could make that mistake any longer."

"I saw him. He was fishing off the end of the dock when it happened. He didn't look happy as he stormed past me on his way to see you."

"The office was pretty busy today with all kinds of

things. He wasn't the only hook in fingers. And a little girl broke her arm, coming down a slide. We had to fix that but she's doing good. Had to send someone to Tampa with an appendicitis attack. For Sunset Bay, it was very eventful."

Jonah grinned. "I guess that's *waaay* different from when you were working trauma in New York, Chicago, and Los Angeles."

"Yeah, a lot different. But I've grown used to the slower pace. I like going home at a decent hour to see this beautiful woman standing at my side. I don't regret my move or miss any of it."

"Good, because we're glad you're here. Did Erin and Nash tell you the news?"

Rosie grinned. "*Yes!* We're so excited for them. They're perfect for each other. And now we have another wedding to plan. That's an exciting problem to have."

Adam put his arm around Rosie's shoulders and hugged her to him. "How about you?" he asked, as they both beamed at Jonah. "When are you going to jump into the fray?"

Everyone seemed to be asking him the same

question. Did it show that he was thinking about it? "When the right person comes along. Don't tell Mom, but I'm about to start looking again, so if you have any ideas, let me know—" His gaze landed on sleek, dark hair through the crowd. He cocked his head to the side and looked past Rosie. *Was this the woman from the pier?* The sudden triple time of his heartbeat told him yes.

"Who do you see?" Adam asked as he and Rosie shifted to the side and followed his gaze.

"I'm not sure." *He needed to take a look at her finger.* "If you'll excuse me, I have something I need to check out." As if drawn by a bungee cord, he moved forward.

"Sure," Adam called.

"Who is he looking at?" Rosie asked Adam.

Jonah knew that they were watching him and in seconds, they'd have their answer. And so would he, if this was his mystery woman.

CHAPTER THREE

Jonah maneuvered through the crowd, saying hello to a few people but not pausing. He was on a mission. He worked his way around, trying to get in an angle where he could see the woman's face. She was talking to Lila Peabody and had her back nearly against the firehouse wall, but she was angled away from him. She held a glass of cola, which would make seeing a ring on her finger a piece of cake. He had almost made it to her when she turned and her eyes met his. *It was her.* Instant heat filled him as her gaze locked on him.

Sparks like fireworks on display on the Fourth of July in New York City exploded inside him. *Whoa.*

Maybe it was because he'd had her on his mind for several days. He still didn't know her name, still didn't know anything about her except he could see her ring finger and there was nothing on it.

Relief hit him. But that didn't automatically mean she wasn't married. He walked through the crowd, straight toward her. Determined to know now whether he had a free and clear on this attraction he was feeling or whether he needed to get her out of his mind once and for all.

Before he reached her, Hunter, the new fireman, walked up and put his arm around her and gave her a brief hug. Jonah's heart tumbled inside his ribs, hitting each one as it plummeted toward his feet. *Was she Hunter's wife? Girlfriend?* He hadn't said anything about one but they'd barely had a conversation.

He watched as Hunter put his hands in his pockets but remained close to her. She smiled up at him and then he said something to her, then to Lila, and they all laughed. Jonah stood frozen, uncertain about what to do. Even if she wasn't taken, he didn't want Lila and her group zeroing in on him. He feared, right now, Lila would be able to look at him and know he was smitten.

As he stood there like a fool, full of questions, she looked back and saw him again. She looked stunned that he was still there and smiled at him. Hunter and Lila both looked his way, too.

"Jonah." Hunter waved him over. "Come here. I'd like to introduce you to my sister."

Sister.

He grinned. Relief, as if he had just gone over Niagara Falls in a barrel and lived, washed over him. He was weak-kneed but still crossed the short distance between them faster than an Olympic sprinter. She was single, and he hadn't compromised his strict belief that a married woman was sacred. He hadn't realized until that moment exactly how bad he had been worried. But now another sensation filled him…hope.

"Hi," he said, still grinning. "We met, unofficially, at the pier a couple of days ago. I'm Jonah Sinclair. It's nice to meet you…" He paused, waiting for her name.

She smiled and slipped her hand into the one he

had held out to her. "I'm Summer Claremont."

Summer. Perfect name because she brightened up his life like a sunny day. He just stared at her as her hand warmed his and the hum of electricity seemed to surround them.

"Jonah is one of our most eligible bachelors," Lila said, instantly reminding Jonah the sassy sixty-year-old was witnessing the entire introduction.

But as Summer's gorgeous emerald eyes captivated him, he didn't care who was near and watching them. He didn't care about anything except that he knew her name, she was single, and her hand felt like warm satin in his hand.

* * *

Summer had hoped she would see Jonah tonight. She both wanted to see him and feared seeing him. She had had him on her mind the last few days, ever since they had talked at the pier. She had wondered about him, even not long after her nightmare two nights ago. Nightmares plagued her, horrified her, and woke her, drenched in the night and sometimes screaming for help. It was awful. Poor Polly and Hunter. They would rush to her room and calm her down. She would see the fear in Polly's eyes and it would make her wonder whether coming here was a good thing or a bad thing. She needed to get over these nightmares; she didn't need to keep frightening Polly. Polly had her own nightmares to deal with. But her dear, sweet niece would soothe her and tell her, "Aunt Summer, it's okay. It's us. It's not those bad people." And then she would hug Summer and kiss her cheek as Summer buried her face in the sweet scent of Polly's hair and hold her tightly.

She shook herself, realizing she'd gotten lost in her head, as she often did these days.

Hunter and Polly were her saving grace right now. And she prayed Hunter hadn't made a mistake, talking her into coming to Sunset Bay with them. They had their own tragedy to overcome without having to deal with hers. But he said Polly needed her as much as she needed Polly and him. So here she was, determined that she would overcome what had happened to her.

Hunter said it would be good for Polly to see her do it, and that made her more determined to beat her demons. She would not let her attacker win. She would not only survive; she wanted to thrive.

Hunter told her to do that, she had to fight. And he wouldn't be happy if she gave up.

Her brother was a firm believer in stretching oneself and reaching goals. He knew about adversity himself. What he had gone through with Polly's mother hadn't been easy, and yet he survived with flying colors—at least, from what she could tell. His iron-clad resolve would have pulled him through.

She had assured him that she was fighting. And that meant that she would meet people unafraid, including men who she found herself attracted to and feared getting to know.

She shook herself again and realized Jonah was still holding her hand and staring at her with a warm but slightly perplexed gaze.

How long had she drifted deep in thought? What had Lila said?

"Hi again." She looked at her brother and at Lila

before looking back at Jonah. She tried to ignore the pattering of her heart and concentrated on the fact that she was being watched by both Hunter and Lila. "I hope you've had a good few days."

His warm and firm grasp still held her hand. Shivers of awareness coursed up through her, not shivers of fear. She hadn't held her hand out to anyone since arriving. Finding ways to avoid a direct touch with anyone was her goal, so why had she almost instantly held her hand out to Jonah?

He suddenly glanced at their hands. "Oh, sorry." As if he had realized he was still holding her hand, he released it.

She was instantly missing it. Which was so odd.

"I have had a good few days. I realized after you left the other day that I hadn't gotten your name. And when I met Hunter, I didn't put together that the sister he mentioned might be you. I'm assuming Polly is Hunter's daughter?"

"Yes. She's my niece."

He grinned. It was a beautiful grin that widened into a smile that lifted his beautiful, gentle eyes.

"Perfect. I wasn't sure if you were married?"

Again, he said the word as a question. "No. Never had the pleasure."

"Me either. Although it seems my family are dropping like flies lately."

That brought laughter from Lila. "It looks like you two are getting along fine and so my suggestion would be that Jonah take you out in a boat and show you around. He knows his way around a boat since he has so many of them and he knows his way around Sunset Bay. Jonah, you should ask this beautiful lady out for a ride, soon. Don't hem-haw around now."

Jonah looked slightly embarrassed and Summer found that endearing. But she was shocked at the idea of going on a date. *Could she?*

"Lila, as a matter of fact, I've already invited Summer and Polly *and* Hunter for a day on the boat. They're all going to let me know when is a good time to go out on the water for them."

She liked this man even better. He had breezed through a potentially awkward situation. "Yes, and that was very nice of you, inviting us. Especially after the way Polly had insinuated herself with you the other day, trapping you with conversation like she had."

"Was no hardship. She's an adorable little girl and I enjoyed talking to her. I enjoy talking to you, too. The offer stands. Although, unlike what Lila is hoping for, you don't have to look at it as a date because I totally get that we just met. You don't know me and eating ice cream cones on the same pier isn't enough time to get to know someone."

"Thank you. It's a very nice offer but it's up to Hunter. We have to make sure Polly would want to go and that she's ready."

"Sure. Hunter, the offer stands—it's totally up to you guys. Anyway, I just wanted to stop by and say hi and now that I have everything straight, I'll leave you all to your conversation."

"Thanks." Hunter had a curious look in his eye that Summer felt a little uneasy about. "We'll talk to Polly and see how she feels about it. But in the meantime, I'm working right now, but in three days my shift is up and I'll be home for a few days and during that time Summer is free to go see whatever she'd like. It would be good for her to get out. So why don't you make a date?" He pinned her with a hopeful look.

Her sweet brother was encouraging her to step out, to push herself. But she also knew he was watching to see whether she would try. They all knew the Sinclairs were a great family. Brad Sinclair was the fire chief—his boss—and they had already heard from several people that they were a great family. She had already been introduced to Mr. and Mrs. Sinclair and several of Brad's brothers, which would be Jonah's family.

One brother, Tate, had said he was just in town briefly and was leaving soon but he had been glad to meet her. He was so amazingly gorgeous—movie star gorgeous—and from what she heard, he was a stunt double for movie stars on several movies. But she hadn't reached her hand out to shake his hand. And when he had smiled at her with amazing eyes, very similar to Jonah's, she had felt nothing but the happiness of meeting someone new in town, and thinking he was a nice person. There had been none of this attraction she felt toward Jonah. Still, she didn't want to go out alone with any man—even Jonah. She was afraid to go.

She wanted to turn him down so badly. But her brother was watching her and they had just had that conversation about her pushing herself. Burying her fears, she nodded. "Okay, I think your first day off is Saturday. Would one of those days be a good day for you to take me out on the boat?"

Jonah smiled. "It would be a perfect day. I'll set it up. We could leave about ten?"

"Sure. Ten sounds perfect." And with that, she had just made a date.

She just hoped she could make it through it.

CHAPTER FOUR

Rosie was glad for a moment of reprieve at her bakery, Bake My Day. Mid-afternoon was sometimes a little slower than the rest of the day and usually by this time, she and her workers needed a moment to recuperate from the busy morning and lunch rush. She was so grateful to have the business but at this moment, since Gigi was out for a dentist appointment and her early morning help had left already, Rosie was happy to fix herself a glass of tea and join the little group of ladies sitting in the corner, chatting away.

It was nice that her place had become the hot spot for the local group of ladies who were involved in everything in Sunset Bay. But they were also the local gossips and though Rosie had never been one to be big on gossip, she had come to realize that having her bakery meant that she was going to know everything there was to know about everyone and there wasn't a lot she could do to avoid it. As long as it wasn't rude or offensive or drifting into private territory, she was fine. And the good thing was none of these sweet ladies seemed to find that kind of gossip entertaining. Thankfully, Sunset Bay wasn't one for vicious gossip. It was usually good-natured and basically trying to be helpful in sometimes odd situations, but mostly it was about who was seeing who, and who could be fixed up with who. She smiled at that because not too long ago, the subject of their fixer-upping was her.

The ladies—Lila, Doreen, Mami, and Birdie—were at the moment discussing her brother-in-law Jonah. And she actually wanted in on that conversation. She and Adam had witnessed exactly what they were talking about right now: his actions at the welcome party at the firehouse for the new fireman, Hunter Claremont. Everyone had hopes that Jonah would be happily married before any of his brothers or sisters. That hadn't happened and then suddenly, as if he had given up on finding love, he stopped dating. Everyone was worried because Jonah was adorable. He was handsome, gorgeous in his own way, and gentle. He would be an amazing husband; he was a fantastic provider with his business that was just going gangbusters. And yet, he wasn't married. But yesterday, she and Adam had witnessed him make a beeline straight through the crowd toward Hunter's sister.

"He looked like a torpedo shooting toward a target, yesterday," Birdie said. "I saw him even from across the crowd. That man was on a mission."

Lila grinned knowingly. "Yes, he was. You should have seen his expression close up. The boy was smitten. He tried to hide it but the man's got no poker face going on. He is an open book."

Mami smirked. "At least to experienced old gals like us." She laughed and so did the rest of them.

"He is so adorable," sweet Doreen said softly. "I could just hug him up. But as short as I am, I'd only be hugging his legs."

Rosie chuckled at that. It was a bit of an exaggerated statement but not by much. Doreen was short, squat, and top-heavy, something she often quipped about.

"Adam and I witnessed it, too, and at first wondered what in the world had gotten his attention, because he had been talking to us and then, boom! He barely excused himself before he raced in her direction."

Lila broke in. "And you should have seen their gazes when they locked with each other's. *Fireworks.* Sparks like a lightning strike. Took my breath away."

"I love it," Mami gushed. "I was not facing so that I could see him, but I saw her and knew instantly that she liked him."

"Yup, it was powerful." Birdie grinned. "Jonah stopped dead in his tracks and then after just a few moments, he interrupted the conversation, it looked like. It had been amazing to watch."

"Yes, it had been." Rosie and Adam had both looked at each other and grinned, hopeful that this could be it. Because they wanted so much for Jonah to find romance and true love.

Everyone looked at her. Then Birdie frowned.

"You look tired," Birdie said. The wiry little lady looked at her with a frank expression. Birdie was known for her bluntness. "You feelin' okay?"

"Birdie, I'm drained. I'm glad for a moment to sit down and listen to you girls."

Lila beamed at her. "New romance always energizes me. And Jonah and Summer especially look interesting since they were both trying to hide or deny their obvious attraction. I can't figure out why. Especially since it was like the Fourth of July in August."

"I was standing over there getting me a piece of German chocolate cake off the dessert stand." Birdie fanned herself with her hand. "It was like a heatwave came across the whole place when they looked at each other. I was riveted—I tell you, I was riveted to the spot as they began to talk. And I was a little jealous that Lila was standing right there beside them, hearing everything."

Rosie chuckled. She had never heard Birdie get so dramatic but she knew exactly what she was feeling because she and Adam had felt it too. It had been amazing.

Mami chortled. "I felt it, too. I wasn't getting any of that wonderful German chocolate cake that Deidra Allen had brought, but I was getting me a glass of punch and I happened to see him stop dead in his tracks and wondered what in the world was this young man doing. I almost felt for a moment like she was caught between a want to and not want to. You know what I mean—a little tug and a little pull. But I was sure hoping she would pull because I wanted to see what was going to happen. And sure enough, he started walking toward her...gives me big old goose bumps just thinking about it. Don't you just *love* love at first sight?"

Rosie gaped at Mami. "Now wait, I'm not so sure you aren't jumping to some conclusions. I mean, I love a good romance but Jonah just met Summer. Maybe you need to dial it back a bit."

Mami looked appalled. "I think not. I know what I saw and I loved it. It was like we were watching a movie, you know? I was hooked. Hooked, I tell you."

Rosie laughed and gave up.

Doreen chuckled. "Mami, you are such a card. *I* was talking to the pastor and I happened to look up and saw the look on sweet Jonah's face. It was like he was in shock, you know? His beautiful eyes of blue steel softened—the boy does not, as Birdie said, have a poker face. He did lock onto her like a heat-seeking missile going for his target as he stormed the ramparts to get to her. I was having palpitations just watching. And I forgot I was talking to the pastor. Poor man had to turn around to see what had me so enthralled."

Rosie almost died laughing but held back, considering it would have embarrassed Doreen. But honestly, she had never heard the shy lady talk so much. Jonah had definitely made an impression and there was no way he was getting out of this without these ladies getting involved.

He had no idea what he'd done at that welcome

party.

Doreen wasn't finished, either. "But I couldn't help ignoring the pastor. Jonah needs a wife, and he needs a wife *bad*. I was so excited I almost jumped up and down—" She giggled. "And you all know if I'd have done that, I would've fallen over because of these big ole boobs of mine. *Sooo,* I didn't jump." A dimple showed among the deep blush.

Rosie about fell off her chair. "Doreen, calm yourself. I have never seen you get so excited. You're usually shy."

Doreen's eyes twinkled. "I know. I can't help myself—it was just the look in his eyes. It was just so romantic. I wish that some man in my long life of nobodies had ever looked at me like that. I guess I was just hopeful for him because I had such a hopeful heart for myself…you know what I mean?"

Rosie did know because she had felt that sense of electricity when she'd first met Adam. She would never forget when he had moved in next to her. She had felt that connection instantly. She wanted everybody to feel that connection. To know that

Doreen had never felt drawn or connected to anyone like that made her heart hurt. The older woman was so sweet, but so shy, like a wallflower that had just matured and had never gotten off the wall. But Doreen was the sweetest thing and she didn't seem as though she minded, at least not enough to ever try to change it.

Rosie took a sip of her tea. "I heard they agreed to a date?" She looked at Lila because Lila had been standing right there when it all happened.

"Yes, they did. They're going on a boat date on Saturday. And her brother helped set it up. It was almost like Jonah was going to walk away without actually asking her out and Hunter stepped in and practically pushed his sister to make a firm date for Saturday. As if he was looking out for his sister and he knew a good guy when he saw it and he was…giving her permission to go out with the guy. I thought it was very sweet. But, you know, if she's almost thirty, if not older than that, it's a bit strange. But anyway, yes, Saturday is the day, and we are so excited. We're thinking about hiding out in a boat and watching them get together on the dock. Just to see if they have that lightning strike look again between them."

The other ladies were nodding and smiling and Rosie felt as if she needed to put a halt to some of this. Because really, who wanted little old ladies spying on them at the dock? Especially when they were getting ready to go on a first date.

"Okay, whoa, ladies. I can understand being excited and everything because Jonah is a fabulous man and we love him to death. But I'm sure hiding out behind a boat or in a boat watching him and Summer is not the right thing to do."

Birdie frowned. "In other words, you're telling us to back off and not have a little excitement in our own lives?"

"Yes, I do believe that is exactly what I said. Come on, you know you can't go following them around."

"Says you," Birdie grunted. "I think it's a good idea. What about you gals?"

Doreen looked down and said nothing now.

Mami smiled sneakily. "I think we can be quiet. Besides, Rosie, you never heard this conversation and as far as you know, we're not going to let you in on what we see or hear. How's that, girls—maybe we don't need to let Rosie in on our little talks anymore because she might try to prevent us from having our little excitement. You know we enjoy this sort of thing."

Rosie gaped at them. Lila was silent, too, but her eyes twinkled with mischief. Rosie narrowed her eyes. "Let me get this straight. You follow people around and watch them? This is a normal practice?" She had never thought this.

Lila waved her hand. "You're getting upset about nothing, Rosie. We have, on occasion, been at certain places when certain people met up for dates. And it's fun. We don't always get to know when people are going to meet but every once in a while, we hear and, well, you know, there's a lot of places to hide and watch."

Rosie thumped her forehead with the palm of her hand. She closed her eyes briefly then opened them and stared at the ladies. "Okay, stop. Please tell me you are not going to continue this sort of thing."

Birdie met her eyes with a frank stare. "We will not tell you such a thing. If we want to follow somebody around and see if they're going to have a little get-together, then we're going to do it. You cannot make us not have our little bit of fun. It's exciting."

What in the world was she witnessing? Should she warn Jonah that he was being watched? Rosie had a dilemma and she really did not know what to do about it. But maybe staying out of it was the best option. Really, what could the ladies do other than snoop? Maybe when Jonah found them or if he happened to see them, he would think it was funny. At least she hoped he would.

CHAPTER FIVE

Saturday morning, Jonah could barely contain his excitement as he waited for Summer to arrive. It had been a long time since he'd anticipated a date more than he was this one. He tried to chalk it up to the fact that he hadn't dated in over a year. But he knew that it wasn't the reason for the way he was feeling. Summer was the reason, and the only reason for this excitement and hope flowing through him.

He wanted to give Hunter a hug the day of the party when he had stepped in and basically had Summer agree to the date. Something had made her cautious and he actually liked that. He wanted to prove himself worthy of her trust. He was so tired of going out just for the sake of going out; he wanted her to feel how special he felt about her agreeing to spend time with him.

In his heart of hearts, he knew this was special.

When he saw her blue Ford drive up into the parking lot, he moved to the dock. He wasn't prepared for the sight of her in modest, mid-thigh white shorts, and a flowing red shirt that covered most of her arms but bared her shoulders as it was pushed slightly off them with an elastic neckline. She was stunning with her glistening, dark hair flowing down her back. And despite the fact that she was probably going to have to pull it back at some point, he was glad that she was wearing it down.

His gaze scanned her long legs and then found her shoes; she'd worn dock shoes, with non-slick soles. She knew something about boating and this made him happy. So many other dates had worn slick-bottomed sandals, and he'd had to keep them from slipping down for most of the trip. He loved being on the water, so taking someone out on it was a natural thing for him to want to do. But he'd become reluctant to do that after a few seemed practically unable to stand up, so much to the point he'd asked them to take their shoes off. Or maybe, he hated to say, but sometimes he thought the whole thing was a ploy by them to get him to hold them. Which sadly, got really old. However, he wouldn't mind the excuse to get to hold Summer. But he wouldn't have that excuse because she had worn the correct shoes.

He held his arm up and waved at her, so she would know which boat to come to. She spotted him and smiled, and his heart lurched in his chest. He smiled as she headed his way. *How had he gotten so lucky*, he wondered, unable to take his eyes off her.

He hoped she was as connected to him as he was to her. He feared that he was getting a little overexcited about the date. Maybe it was because it had been so long since he had dated but his heart of hearts had told him that wasn't it. Something about Summer was different from anyone he had ever dated and it had been good that he had waited for her to show up in his life. He liked that thought; he liked it a lot.

She walked down the dock toward him, her hips swaying slightly, her hair swinging with it. Her gaze locked on his as she got closer. His heart pounded harder the closer she got, sounding as if a thousand horses were trampling through him. He couldn't take his eyes off her, riveted on her, loving every moment. He wanted to kiss her. He hadn't wanted to kiss a woman in a long time but he wanted to kiss Summer. He wanted to feel her in his arms; he wanted to see her looking at him after he kissed her breathless.

He yanked his thoughts away from the idea of that.

He needed to just make her feel comfortable and happy and have a wonderful time today. It had nothing to do with him wanting to kiss her. That wasn't going to happen for a while. He just hoped she hung around long enough to get to the kissing part. Because something about the look of her, despite her smile, told him that she was ready to run at any moment. And he wondered why.

"You made it. Come on board. I've got everything

ready." He held his hand out to her as she reached him.

"Great." She took his hand.

Electricity sparkled through them like a live wire had just been cut loose from the line. He held her hand securely as she stepped from the dock to the boat. He was ready to catch her just in case she slipped but she was sure-footed. He didn't know whether to approve of that or mourn it. Because if she hadn't been so sure-footed, he was sure he could've pulled her against him when he had caught her. But he would rather her be safe.

"Are you ready to have some fun?" he asked.

"I'm ready. But I have to tell you that it has been a little while since I've been on a boat and, it's a little bit daunting."

What about being on a boat was daunting? She did look a little bit frightened, he realized. He needed to fix that and fix it soon.

"You just hang with me and you'll be fine. You've got great shoes so you should be okay walking around. Even if the deck gets wet, you should be fine. Nothing to worry about, I promise."

"I believe you. Where are we going to go today?"

He grinned. "We're going to go dolphin watching and I'm going to show you some small islands where there's a lot of pelicans that hang out and a lot of different types of fish that show up in the clear water. You never really know what you're going to see. I've seen a lot of pelicans there and sea turtles. You never know. But something good will be there, I'm almost positive."

"That sounds wonderful. I have to tell you that Hunter has been worried about me, and he's been wanting me to get out of the house so much. That was his one worry about when I came to be the nanny— that I wouldn't get out and visit with people enough. I had to promise him that on my days off I would mingle and that some days when I had Polly, we would go out and explore. Which was one reason we were on the dock that day. She loves the ice cream at that place and people-watching. As you should know."

He laughed. "She was cute. And I could tell she and I share both a passion for ice cream and people-watching."

"She must have recognized a kindred spirit." She looked around. "This is fantastic. I've been on boats before but not a yacht."

"Not hardly a yacht, but it is comfortable. It is one of our bigger models and it is a luxury model. You have these captain seats that are real cushy up there on the platform and there's a lot of space, as you can see, in the cabin below. Also, there's a restroom below. I've prepared some snacks, too, and they're in the galley. We could have lunch and just enjoy the day. I don't know if you brought a swimsuit, but if you want to sunbathe or go for a swim in the water, I know great places for that. We can drive way out, as far or as little as you are comfortable going. You're in charge of how far offshore you want to go. We can ride along the coast and pull up to one of my favorite places and have lunch or dinner, if you'd prefer not to have lunch on the boat. I'm very open to anything. This is your day, basically." He was rambling but wanted to make her comfortable.

She stared at him as if stunned, and he figured he'd said too much. "Is that okay?"

"Yes." She laughed, her eyes twinkling. "It sounds fabulous. Great, actually. You've thought of everything. I wasn't sure what we were going to do, so I wore a suit under this outfit. I'm just excited about going out on the water. It's been awhile—really, too long."

Relief made him relax. "I was afraid I was trying too hard and scared you off." He grinned. "Where did you say you were from?"

"I'm impressed, really. And I was raised in Destin. But it's been a long time since I lived there, so I really missed this beautiful blue water. Houston is near Galveston but the water isn't like this."

"We do have some beautiful coastline. Follow me and we'll stow your things below."

He led the way into the cabin and showed her where to put her things, then showed her the cabin of the boat. It was very nice with teak and a little kitchen and a bath and small bedroom, which he told her she could use to change; he wanted her to feel free to use the bottom area any time she wanted to. They got situated and she looked expectantly out toward the ocean as they pulled away from the docks.

"So, where are we going?" She laughed when he looked at her. "I'm just joking. You don't have to repeat your plans."

She was funny. "Open sea? Or down the coast? You have to make a decision. If you choose the island, that's where we will almost be guaranteed to find some dolphins or all the other sea life I mentioned. Sea turtles, pelicans, who knows what may show up. They like the small island that I like, so I see them often—"

"Let's do that," she broke in. "You said we have lunch on board. See how it goes."

"Sounds good to me. Have a seat and here we go."

She sat down and he pushed the throttle. The three powerful boat engines kicked in and they headed out to open water at a fast clip. Excitement hummed between them as they glanced at each other and he saw a kindred spirit in loving the water.

He knew so little about her but he was infatuated with her.

"You seem so at ease on the water," he said over the wind. The breeze lifted Summer's hair and it fluttered behind her, and she didn't seem to care that it was going to be tangled.

"Yes. My family lives on the water. I even ran my own boat sometimes. So yes, I'm very used to the water…it's just been awhile. Thank you so much for asking me. I've been needing this."

He heard the emotion in her voice and he wondered whether there was more to her story. "Well, I'm glad I was able to do something you needed."

They both stared out across the water as more space disappeared behind them.

"Is that the island?" She stood and looked out over the glass shield on the boat, pointing.

"Yes, that's it. A pretty little jewel out here in paradise."

He eased the boat as close to the small island, as was safe. "We'll anchor out here and use the dinghy to go ashore."

"Perfect."

He found his spot and they gathered up things from the galley that he had brought for lunch—chicken salad sandwiches, some strawberries, and key lime pie—and placed them in the insulated carry bag. He pushed a button and lowered the small dinghy to the water, then helped her climb in from the rear of the vessel.

When they were settled, he started its little motor and took off toward shore. He went slowly. As they were driving along, she spotted the first stingray. It was shiny gray as it swam—sailed, basically—over the top of the water and then dove deep. The water was so clear and the rock around the island left pockets where the underwater wildlife loved to hang around. Colorful fish were everywhere.

She looked from the water to him. "This is amazing."

"I love it. I'm glad you do too." He liked that she enjoyed the ocean like he did. It was one more thing about her that attracted him to her.

"I love it too. I could spend hours just doing this. It's so…calming and exciting at the same time."

"Exactly," he said.

She was amazing and he was totally and completely captivated by her

It was almost too good to be true.

CHAPTER SIX

Summer had enjoyed the ride so much. Being on the water took her back to growing up and the carefree days of life in Destin, in a small area outside the town. She'd loved it but always dreamed of being a career woman with a job in Houston. Or New York.

When she had taken the commercial art job in Houston, it had been a dream come true. She had had an offer in New York, too, and being young, she had really considered it. But Houston had been a little bit closer, so she decided that she could always, after she developed her career some, hopefully move up to a job in New York if she wanted. Now she couldn't even imagine it. At all.

But this was what she needed and as long as she kept focused, she was doing great. And Jonah was so mild-mannered and just so easy to be with that she hadn't panicked yet. She was watching her every move carefully so as not to trigger a panic attack. And while they were flying across the water in the boat and he had his hands on the wheel, she had relaxed. She had almost told him a little bit about herself but had stopped before she had said too much.

Jonah was easy to talk to but she wasn't ready to open the door to her past.

When they reached the island shore, he hopped out and tugged the dinghy onto the sand. He took her hand as she stepped into the ankle-deep water. It swirled around her legs and it felt so wonderful. There was nothing like the feel of warm ocean water and soft sand between your toes.

She smiled, feeling lighthearted for the first time in so long. "It's wonderful. We may have to take a swim. I'd love to bring Polly out here sometime.

Although, like I said, Hunter has to feel comfortable about it."

He tugged the boat to the sand far enough from the water that it was secure and then he lifted the basket from it and carried it farther up the small shore. "Is there a problem with Polly? A couple of times, you seemed worried about her in the water and the boat?" He pulled the blanket from the basket.

She reached for one side of it, her emotions conflicted. *Should she tell him?* "Polly..." She hesitated. "She and her mother were in a boating accident about three years ago. Polly was very young and survived but her mother didn't. It was horrible. Polly had her life vest on and when they were thrown into the water, the life vest is what saved her from drowning. But, her mother, who was a very experienced boater, didn't have one on and she hit her head. She drowned." Even now, it was hard to talk about.

He stared at her.

"It didn't take long for rescue teams to get to them," she continued. "They weren't that far out, but for some reason or another, she ran the boat into the rocks. It was devastating and Polly, though she was barely three, remembers it. And though she's been near the water, she's never been on the water again. But she is infatuated by all things involving water. I don't know how successful we'll be getting her on a boat. We're not pushing her. I think when she's ready, she'll let us know. Although, you know that saying—it's always better to get back on the horse after getting thrown—this is not the same. Life and death negate simple sayings. It's not as easy as it sounds. Nor is it actually important that she ever get back in a boat."

"I am so sorry." Jonah looked shocked, stunned. "Poor Polly. Thank God she had her life vest on." He stared at her, questions in his eyes. "And you—that statement about getting back on the horse not being easy. You said that as if you have first-hand experience with that. Is there more?"

Why had she started this conversation? Why hadn't she just let it be about Polly? "A little bit. But I'm not having as easy an experience as I hoped getting back on the horse. But I'm getting there."

He straightened and then reached for the picnic basket and set it on the blanket. He put his hands on his hips and studied her. "I'm sorry to hear you're having trouble with something. That must be difficult. Is it anything I can help with?"

"Actually, you are helping a little bit. See, I'm here on this island with you. Out in the middle of nowhere. That's huge for me."

*　*　*

Jonah stared at Summer. "I don't understand what you're saying."

She looked uncomfortable. He hadn't meant to make her uncomfortable but he was curious about the statement. Really curious. She looked stricken now, as if worried about something. He hadn't meant to bring her out here and bring up something unpleasant. He'd wanted her to have a good time.

"Do I need to take you home? You look upset."

She crossed her arms across her waist and moistened her lips. "Look, I was attacked. In the garage of the building I worked at in Houston. I was going to my car. I fought and thankfully managed to not be harmed in that way, although I suffered some facial bruises and things of that sort. But, thank God, a man heard me screaming and came to my defense and he wasn't afraid to fight. The man who attacked me is now in jail. But it's, umm…it's left me feeling more vulnerable than I've ever felt in my life. And I have nightmares."

Jonah felt sick to his stomach. "I can't believe this. I'm so sorry."

She had a blank look to her expression as she continued, "I came here because I couldn't go back to my job and thankfully my employers understood. I'm hoping to be able to work part-time for them soon, from the house. In the meantime, I watch Polly and I work on overcoming this feeling of violation that I can't seem to shake. And I hate it. I despise it, but I'm unable to shake it."

She blinked really hard and he saw tears glistening in her eyes as she turned away from him to stare out at the water. Unable to stop himself, he moved behind her and placed a comforting hand on her shoulder.

Instantly, she screamed and swung around, gasping. Her face held a look of horror as she raised her hands and backed away from him. Her eyes were wide with fear. Jonah froze. She was breathing hard, shallow gasps coming from her. Tears streamed down her face.

"Summer. I'm sorry, I didn't mean to scare you." He backed away and held his hands at his side, trying to seem non-threatening. "I'm not going to hurt you. Breathe. Easy now."

She took a deep breath and seemed to get hold of herself but her eyes looked so sad. "No, I'm sorry. I forgot and turned my back on you. I should have told you. I can't have anyone come up behind me. I lose control." Tears continued to stream. She wiped them away with her fingers, anger contorting her beautiful face.

His heart broke for her.

"It makes me so mad, so angry that I still react this way. I guess I'll go the rest of my life not being able to turn my back on someone because I'm afraid that they're going to walk up behind me. I can't even turn my back on Polly. Little Polly. It's like I go to this place and I can't stop myself. I'm just instantly back in that dark garage—he's got his hands around my mouth and around my body."

He stood where he was but he wanted to hold her. To tell her it was going to be okay. He stood right where he was, not sure what to do next. "You're going to get through this. You are strong. You're just vulnerable right now. You're going to get through it. You're safe right now. See, it's just me and I'm not behind you. I'll never approach you from behind like that again. You're going to be okay."

He reached down to the picnic basket, pulled out a napkin and held it out to her. "Here—use this for your tears. And then come over here and sit down and let me pour you something to drink so you can relax and calm down."

She took the napkin from him then dabbed at her tears, sniffed and followed him to the blanket. He moved to the far side and sank down to his knees and then pulled out the thermos of sweet tea. He poured her a glass and held it out to her. She sank to the blanket on the other side of the picnic basket and looked embarrassed. *She had been through the wringer.* Her fingers trembled as she took the glass from him and lifted it to her lips to sip from it.

"Do you go to counseling?" He watched her, worried for her.

"I do, but I haven't had a meeting with the counselor in the area yet. We have an appointment set up for two days from now."

"Good. Maybe with counseling you can overcome this. And honestly, this is a great town. Once people know what's happened to you, they'll come around you and they'll watch out for you. They'll do everything they can to not do anything that causes you pain like I just did."

She gripped the plastic glass and swallowed hard. "I don't want to tell anyone. I can't believe I told you. I haven't told anyone. It's just so personal and there are so many questions when people know."

"I understand that but you don't know Sunset Bay. There's a lot of friends for you here who wouldn't judge you. I mean, no one would judge you for what happened to you. And I can see where you would be afraid of questions—I can see how that would be a problem. Is discussing it really hard on you?"

She nodded. "Normally. I don't know why but I feel I can talk to you. I have no clue why and I'm sure you wish I would stop talking. I'm sure this is making you uncomfortable too."

He frowned. "No, not at all. I would like to help you in any way I can. If you want to talk to me, that's great. I'm just so, so sorry this happened to you. I don't mean to ask questions but is this guy…is he still in jail? He did go to jail, I hope?"

"He is and he's going to serve time. They didn't let him out. He had prior convictions. This was not his first attack. I have going to trial to look forward to. I have to go face him. Because I did press charges. I might be suffering emotionally because of what he did or attempted to do, how bad he hurt me. But I didn't back down from pressing charges. I'll do whatever it takes to put him behind bars so he can't do this to anyone else."

"I applaud you for that. See—you are strong. He didn't take that away from you." He tried to encourage her while wishing he could rip this guy's head off. Anger boiled inside him.

Her expression was so sweet with relief. Then she looked at him and his gut twisted; he wanted so badly to put his arms around her. To hold her and tell her it was going to be okay. But he didn't dare. Summer Claremont needed to be handled carefully. Her heart was very delicate right now and he had no intention of being anything other than her friend. He wanted to help her get through this and he would not do anything that would make her life feel more vulnerable.

"When do you go to trial?" he asked, even more worried for her now.

She took a deep breath. "I think, unless it gets pushed back again—which it has been pushed back a lot of months for some strange reason, but they just keep finding more things about him and I don't really know the law—but I'm hoping at the end of the month when we're supposed to go to trial that it happens and you know, maybe once there's closure on that, then I can get the closure I need in my life to be me again."

He hoped so too, very much so. "Well, unless you want to keep talking and tell me whatever you need to tell me, I just want you to know that I'm here for you. I'm officially your first new friend and I want to do whatever I can to help you, okay?"

She nodded. "I'd like that."

He did too. "Then let's eat and then we'll do whatever you want to do. We're not going to let that guy ruin our day. How's that sound?"

She took a deep breath and pushed her shoulders back. She blinked any remaining tears from her eyes and swallowed hard as he watched her.

"I think that sounds like a plan. I'm tired of him taking my beautiful days and ruining them."

He smiled, hoping to help. "Then let's do this."

CHAPTER SEVEN

Summer was uncomfortable but she had told him what had happened to her and for her, it was actually an accomplishment. However, she wasn't exactly sure why she had told him. Probably because he was so earnest. Or, would she say that he was just calming; something about him had drawn her from the beginning and gave her confidence in him. She had never felt that before, not so quickly, with anyone. And then for her to spill her guts to him basically after he had about scared her to death... Poor man—she'd probably frightened him.

But as she sank down onto the blanket and accepted the sandwich and the cheese tray that he set before them, she felt herself calm. Her pulse had gotten back to a normal pace and when he smiled at her, the panic eased and her heart lifted. She responded with a smile at him. He was right; they weren't going to let her attacker take their day away. And now that he knew what her problem was, she was certain he wouldn't startle her again.

It dawned on her then that when she was with him, he would prevent anyone else from doing the same. Hunter did that for her at the party at the firehouse the other night. She had approached the crowd from the side and then found a wall and stood with her back to it. This minimized her worry about anyone approaching from behind her. And when they were leaving, Hunter always walked slightly behind her, where she could see him but where he could play guard for her. Now, even though he hadn't signed up for the job, she knew Jonah would be watching out for her too. Especially if she asked him. He would protect her and he seemed to have confidence that anyone else in town who knew about her problem would do the same. But there was no way the entire town could know. She just wasn't comfortable telling everyone. Maybe, in time, as she got to know everyone more and more, she could do that. But not right now.

Maybe if she got to know Jonah's family, then she would feel comfortable with them knowing. She would just have to see. But for now, she took a bite of the sandwich.

"Did you make this? It's great."

"I did make it, from my mom's recipe for chicken salad. I'm crazy about it. When I moved out of the house, I had her teach me how to make it. Of course, she made sure her boys knew how to cook before we left home. My brothers rebelled on this recipe, though, because it has a lot of extra steps to it. Like peeling the grapes before you put them in. That's her added touch."

Shocked, Summer looked at the sandwich and sure enough, there was the skinless grape. "Oh my goodness, you peeled the grapes. You really did."

He laughed. "Yes, I did. They are slippery little

devils, too. And just so you know, I don't share my chicken salad with just anybody."

She could not believe the trouble he'd gone to. "I feel very, very special. Thank you. I'll have to make something that my mom taught me to make and share it with you. Payback, you know, isn't always terrible. And you are getting paid back. After what I've put you through today, you really deserve it."

"I can't wait. After I nearly scared you to death, I'd be very happy to have my payback be you agreeing to go back out with me?" He hitched a brow.

"Maybe. But I hope you understand how cautious I am about dating."

"I get it. Let's just say, I'd be grateful for you to spend time with me. Friends?"

"Yes." She smiled and took another bite of the sandwich. It was delicious. They ate for a little while, talking some about the island and how long he had been coming here and how he had found it when they were in high school and motoring about on the boats and that it was a place that he and his whole family enjoyed coming but nobody ever got out here very often. Like he said, nobody was ever here and it was almost as if it were their own little private spot in the middle of the ocean.

"I'm glad you shared this with me."

"My pleasure. Look, I have to tell you something. Maybe warn you. I haven't been on a date in so long that you're probably going to draw attention from several people in town and you'll probably be wondering why these people are paying so much attention to you. It may be mostly because you're beautiful and new in town, but it *might* be partly because people are nosey, especially some of the ladies in town. My mom and my sisters-in-law are included in that. When you see them, they might be grinning a little bit bigger than normal and it will be because of this outing with me."

"I guess that means they're glad you asked me out?"

"Yes, very glad. And word around here spreads like wildfire. It's not like it's really terrible gossip but I knew the minute I asked you out, people would know. But you know what? I don't care. I've been wanting to ask you out since that first day we saw each other on the pier."

"Really?" She didn't tell him that he'd been on her mind since that same day.

"Yes. And then the second time I saw you sitting on the pier painting I almost came over then—I just realized how you were positioned that day—you had pulled up a little stool with your back to the sea wall there and facing the dock. You were sitting so no one could come up from behind you. Wow, I see that now. But I didn't pick up on it until now. Were you painting the marina?"

"I was. I'm a commercial artist and I really enjoy it. I paint with all kinds of mediums, including on the computer. But oils are my first love, my medium that's good for my soul. I felt drawn to pull the oils out and just paint what pleased me, not a client. The marina called to me. It's beautiful—a very quintessential small, beach town. And you've got a very wonderful assortment of different types of boats that make it interesting. The topaz water, with the different colorful boats—yellows, reds—and then the docks with the people. And then the pelicans.

"Oh, my goodness, there's that one pelican that seems to sit on that main post down there on the end of the pier and it watches everything. I was out there on the pier the other day and I could swear that same pelican was watching me. He's got a tuft of feathers on his head that's a little unusual. He was sitting atop that building, you know, on the end, checking things out."

Jonah laughed. "That's Seymour. He sees everything…more than anyone, so thus his name."

She laughed. "Seymour. I love it."

"He's an old sailor, that one. He's been around for a long time. He's got just that look about him, kind of like he's a rusty old man. You know what I mean?" "Yes, exactly—put a sailor hat on him and yeah, that's what he looks like. And I swear, he looks at me and he looks pretty wise."

"I agree. Anyway, watch out for him. They say he knows who your match is before you do."

"Really?"

"That's what they say. He sees more than meets the eye."

She stared at him. He grinned. "You're kidding me."

"Maybe but there are a lot of stories of when he was around, you'll meet your true love. It happened to Adam and Rosie, and to Brad and Lulu. And Nash remembered seeing him several times from his balcony before he and Erin got together.

"Not to scare you but I saw him the other day too, right before I saw you."

He winked at her, clearly kidding her, but a shiver of delight rushed through her. Jonah was a delight. Everything about the man was just nice. And he was very enjoyable to look at, too. "I saw him *twice* before I saw you," she said, going along with his teasing, despite knowing she wasn't looking for an actual relationship. She was looking for a friend. Friend only.

That's all she could do right now. Maybe ever.

He cocked his head, his eyes still teasing. "Twice? Oh boy, then I think you and me may as well just pack up our bags and head to the church."

Heat suddenly stung her cheeks. She had walked right into that.

His grin grew wider with each rising of the blush on her face. "You look pretty in pink."

"Thank you." It hit her then and she bit her lip and met his gaze. "I fear that going to church is not going to happen anytime soon. Or maybe ever. I actually wonder if I'll be able to overcome this attack enough to ever marry. Not to be a downer again but it's worrisome, you know?"

His expression turned serious, as if trying to will confidence into her. "Summer Claremont, you *will* marry one day. You are an overcomer—I see it in you. I know that you don't need a relationship right now; you need a friend. I swear, from this day forward, I'm your friend and I'll do anything I can to help you get over the trauma you've been through. I like your smile and I'd like to see more of it."

Her heart raced and clenched a little at his words. And somewhere deep, deep in the darkness that seemed to churn inside her soul these days, she saw a glimmer of light.

She hoped with all of her heart that it was the light at the end of the tunnel.

CHAPTER EIGHT

Jonah was on the docks the day after he and Summer had gone out on the boat. He had had her on his mind pretty much nonstop, but nothing had changed about that since he had first spotted her on the pier that first day. Nothing except now, he wasn't just wondering about her; he knew he liked her. And he admired her for what she was working so hard to overcome. He felt for her and if he could've gotten his hands on the guy who had hurt her, he would've hurt him. One look into those tear-filled eyes of Summer's and he'd wanted revenge.

He was working on an old boat today, using his hands and his muscle scrubbing the hull of an old boat in order to alleviate his frustrations. He wasn't paying attention to who was coming down the dock until he heard footsteps behind him and a familiar voice.

"Well, well, Jonah Sinclair, aren't you one handsome man. I tell you what, you need to go around more often without that shirt on."

He closed his eyes and sighed before he turned around, feeling slightly embarrassed because he didn't have his shirt on and Mami Desmond and her three cohorts—Lila, Birdie, and Doreen—stood there, grinning at him. "Mami. Ladies. How are you all doing today?"

Birdie had a little boat that the ladies liked to go out in and do some "fishing" in the bay. They didn't go out very often and they didn't go out far, just right there in the bay so if they were to get into any trouble someone was near to rescue them. Birdie's dinghy wasn't much bigger than she was, so it wasn't going far. He suspected that they used it to spy on people they were trying to be sneaky about. He saw them many times with their binoculars and they were always pointed toward shore or toward a boat. Not at the water.

When they came by, going to the boat, they normally hassled him a little bit. He was usually inside the building and had his clothes on. But today—nope, that wasn't the case. And he had a very, very strong hunch it was him they'd come to spy on.

"I wouldn't tell him to put his shirt on either." Birdie winked at him from beneath her oversized straw hat. It had seen better days, as had her checkered fishing shirt that looked as if it had been her long-dead husband's, with its frayed edges and pearled snaps. She was covered up from head to toe from the sun and carried her fishing poles in one hand. She squinted at him and grinned. "I have to say it's been a long time since I've seen you scrubbing away at something like that. What's got you so riled up? You thinking hard about something?"

"Now, Birdie, you and Mami both lay off this young man," Lila said. "He's just out here working, and I don't mind seeing him out here without his shirt on."

"I agree. You shouldn't give him a hard time. Look at him, he's blushing under that dark tan of his." Doreen—shy, short, and kind of shaped like a cork—smiled sweetly at him.

He smiled back at her and still wished he had his shirt on.

Lila grinned. "You know we're teasing. Sort of." Her eyes twinkled mischievously. "So, how did you and that gorgeous Summer Claremont's boat date go yesterday? I heard y'all spent a long time out there and were both smiling when you got off that yacht you were on."

He grabbed a rag and wiped his hands off so he at least had his hands in front of his chest a little bit. Everybody was watching him with anticipation in their eyes. He had no doubt that they had come today to ride in the boat just so they could find him on the dock to question him about his date with Summer. "Well, ladies, yes, I did take Summer out on the boat. Come to find out, she grew up in Destin and she knows how to handle a boat. We had a really good time." No sense denying it.

"Great," Birdie said. "We heard something bad happened in their past. Do you know what it was?"

"I think she's an artist or something, too," Mami said. "So why is she here being a nanny to her niece?"

He would not answer that. It wasn't his story to tell. "I don't know what you heard but I don't see anything wrong with her coming to watch over her niece. I think it's nice of her. From what I understand, she's a commercial artist and then she paints, too. I think that's really cool."

"I think it is, too," Doreen said. "And I really think it's nice that you took her out. You know, show her around, kind of let her see the sights…get her out of the house a little bit. I just think you're so sweet and I think that is just wonderful of you. I'm sure she just appreciated it a lot."

"Miss Doreen, it was nice. You know me, I'll use any excuse to get out on a boat and I enjoyed very much taking her out. So, about that boat, are y'all going out today?" *Hint, hint*.

He figured they already got what they wanted

from him and he was ready to head in and out of the danger zone. He'd probably be a hot topic down at the bakery this evening or tomorrow. But he hadn't given away anything—just the facts.

He hadn't given away that he was crazy about Summer Claremont, not yet anyway. But the more time they spent together, the more people were going to see straight through his feelings.

Lila sidled over to him and patted his arm. "All that scrubbing on that big boat you're doing sure does build strong muscles. I'm sure Summer will like that."

He was not taking the bait on that one. He didn't have any idea whether Summer liked his muscles or not. He hoped she did. He knew he was intimidating-looking and though he didn't work out like a lot of guys did, he worked out with his work. The physical labor he loved naturally kept him in shape. One thing he wasn't was a glamour boy.

"The boat. Are you going out on it?" he asked again.

"Yes, we're going out on the boat." Birdie held up her rods. "I'm gonna go catch me some fish. I'm having a craving for some seafood tonight."

"If you need anything, all you've got to do is toot that horn of yours and somebody will come running. Good luck."

Mami grinned at him. "We already did. We saw you, didn't we?"

He closed his eyes and groaned. And then he laughed as they waved good-bye and headed off toward their little boat. He turned back to his scrubbing, thankful they were gone.

He wondered how they'd heard all the information that they had. Wondered who else knew that something had happened to Summer. Hunter must have told somebody; he wouldn't doubt if Hunter had told Brad, but he didn't see his brother talking. Brad was real private about other people's business. He knew enough about having his own life gossiped about for years after his fiancée ran off and left him at the altar. After being the main topic of conversation for a long time, Brad wasn't one to talk. Then who?

He thought about little Polly. Yeah, Polly probably knew and being so young, she could have mentioned it to somebody or said some little something that made somebody wonder. He figured that was his best bet right now because he couldn't see Hunter telling anybody who wouldn't keep his business confidential.

Summer didn't want word out about what had happened to her out there, but, despite their nosey ways, he knew if the ladies knew what had happened, they would be her number one support. They really did have good hearts. They would have done everything in their power to help her and protect her.

So would he.

* * *

"You haven't told me how your boat ride with Jonah went the other day?" Hunter asked Summer a couple of days after her boat ride with Jonah.

"It was good. It could have gone badly, though. He came up behind me when we were standing on this little beach and I freaked out. Sometimes I'm afraid I'll never get over being so skittish. I hate it."

Hunter put his arm around her and hugged her. "I'm so sorry. You'll get over it. You will."

She clasped her lip between her teeth, thinking about it. "I hope so. He was really nice about it. He apologized and Hunter...I ended up telling him almost everything. I didn't tell him exactly how bad I had been injured but I told him most of it. That, you know, at least I was injured, and he was really upset about it. After we talked about it and everything, he gave me some encouragement. He also said when he was around, he would do what you do; he would have my back. And he basically told me he would be my friend. He was very empathetic and it was nice."

"See, that's all progress." He picked up the scraper and opened the barbeque pit. When she didn't answer, he glanced up at her.

She swallowed hard. "I guess so. I'd calmed down by then and we ate lunch. And then we rode down the coast and he showed me some landmarks. I really enjoyed it. He encouraged me to tell more people. But I'm not ready."

"You stepped out of your comfort zone. That's the

first time you've told anyone other than me, right? Well, Polly knows some of it."

"Yes, and I told him it was the first time. He was very glad that something about him calmed me enough that I could tell him."

"Do you like him?"

And there was the question she had been waiting for. "I like him as a friend. And I made that clear."

He had started scraping the BBQ pit, getting the grill ready for the burgers. Now he set it down and was quiet for a minute.

She really didn't know what else to say.

"Summer, I'm worried about you. I hope maybe he's the one who can help you past this fear. But I'm not rushing you. You're going to go to your counselor in a couple of days and I've heard he's really good. Talk to him about this. We're going to keep concentrating on getting you healthy. At least healthy enough to go into that courtroom and do what you feel led to do. I, for one, just don't understand why you have to go subject yourself to this."

"I need to do it."

"I guess. If you say so. But if you're going to go, we have to make sure that emotionally you can get through it."

She was relieved he wasn't going to pressure her. "Okay. I'm going to make it through it. I may break down and it may set me back, but I'm going to do this. I have to do it."

"Fine but I'll be right there beside you. And if that judge would let me get at that guy, he wouldn't be standing long."

"Thanks for the sentiment but we're not going to go there. I don't want you ever getting in trouble because of that man. He isn't worth it. You have Polly to think about. She is your priority, not me."

Hunter smiled then, his eyes full of concern. He worried about her and he had enough worries without her stacking more on him. He looked resolved, because he knew it was true. He couldn't do anything to jeopardize his guardianship of his daughter.

She laid a hand on his arm and smiled up at him. "I know you love me, brother. And I'm so grateful for it. And I thank you for bringing me here. I like this little town. Polly does too. We're going to go back to the pier tomorrow and get an ice cream. She wants to go down and look for a manatee, too. We heard that they're there a lot of times or around some of the smaller piers. So, we'll get our ice cream and go looking around. Jonah actually told me a couple of good places to go look."

"I like you and Polly just hanging out, relaxing and enjoying these beautiful days here while you both heal on the inside. It's good for your mental health. I'm glad you came with me."

"I am too. I've been wanting a change, anyway, even before this happened. And I can actually see myself here for a very long time. I don't know what I was thinking that I ever wanted to go live in the city. I tried it and I was managing but my heart was always near the water."

He wrapped an arm around her. "Here's to new beginnings. Huh, sis?"

She laid her head on his shoulder. "Yes, new beginnings."

CHAPTER NINE

Mid-week, Brad stopped by Jonah's office. "Are you ready?"

Jonah looked up from the computer and grinned. "I'm always ready. Are you? Is Tate going to make it back in time?"

Brad leaned against the doorframe. "I think so. I talked to him just a little while ago and he said to count him in. So, the week after next, the Sinclair boys are ready to race. It's a go."

Sunset Bay had a sailboat race every year. The brothers had competed in it all the time when they were growing up but after Adam left for medical school and then Tate had headed off on his many adventures, they weren't able to do it anymore. Jonah had continued to compete with a crew of his employees but this year the brothers had all decided that if they could get home for it, they'd race together. Considering Tate was the only one of the four of them who wasn't living in town these days, it made it a lot easier. And Jonah was excited that he planned to fly back in from the movie set he was working on. Jonah was hyped up they'd all be competing again.

He grinned. "That's awesome. I've got the boat ready. *Sunset Rising* is going to get out there and sail us to victory."

Brad grinned. "Nothing like having a brother who has access to all kinds of boats."

It was pretty cool. "I have to admit that some of my wealthier boarders have offered me to head the crews on theirs, but I wanted to do this with us. And I think our little sailboat has a chance. She's not as big as some of them but she's swift and I think that will be good. If everybody's got their sea legs under them and remembers their duties, then we'll be okay. We'll at least make a good showing."

"And we'll have fun. Mom and Dad are excited. The whole town is. The Sinclair boys are back together. Speaking of having a good time and all that good stuff, how was your date?"

Everybody wanted to know about his date. He sighed. "Brad, it was great. Summer is an amazing person and I am infatuated with her. But she is not ready to date anybody seriously, so I hope the town doesn't get their panties in a wad hoping that I'm going to fall in love and get married next week, because I'm not. We're just friends enjoying each other's company. I sure am hoping that people don't hound her."

Brad's laughter echoed in the large metal building. "I think you like this girl a lot. If I'd known you were talking about getting back in the dating game, I would have had you getting serious about somebody, I would've suggested it a long time ago. I wouldn't have shielded you from Mom and Dad so many times."

"You didn't shield me from Mom and Dad."

Brad laughed again. "None of us could shield one another. But seriously, I won't hound you. I was just curious. Remember, I saw you zero in on her the other night at the party and I hadn't seen you look at anybody like that in forever. Maybe ever."

"Yeah, you're right. Hunter is a good guy and I'm glad he took this job and moved here and brought her to town." He almost said it was good for her, but he held back. He wasn't going to share her story with anybody. He had promised her; it was her story—nobody else's—to tell.

Especially not him.

* * *

Summer took Polly to another small pier on Thursday. They had been checking them out the last few days, looking for manatees. This one was farther away from the main area of town, in a little inlet. They had walked out on the small pier in hopes that today they'd see a manatee.

"You say these are cows of the sea?" Polly looked

at the blue water, her expression full of excitement.

Summer hoped today they would see one. She knew her niece wanted to see what in the world a "cow of the sea" looked like.

Summer laughed. "Yes. It's because they're really big and they have little legs—not that cows have little legs—but cows eat grass, hay, and grain. Vegetation is basically all they eat. Same with a manatee. They live off vegetation in the water."

Summer saw a shadow in the water and sure enough, a manatee surfaced and swam right for them. "Look, Polly, look—do you see?"

Polly squealed. Her face lit up and she jumped up and down. "Is that it? Is that what it looks like?"

"That's it."

"It's so cute. He's big. Oh, he's got the cutest little mouth. Look at him nibble on that plant. And look, Aunt Summer, there's one of his little feet. His feet are not much bigger than my hand." Polly held her hand out.

"You're right. He's adorable."

The large manatee lumbered through the water

right up to the pier, giving Polly a close-up view as he nibbled on the plants near the pier.

"He has a funny tail," Polly said. "It's a flapper."

Summer smiled. "Not exactly like a cow's, is it?"

Polly looked up at her and frowned. "Aunt Summer, I don't see how it looks like a cow at all. It doesn't even have ears."

"I totally know what you're saying."

"I think he looks like one of those black animals— you know, like one of those ones that smack their flippers together and plays ball with you. What are they called?"

"A seal?"

"Yes, you took me to that aquarius," she said slowly, because she had trouble pronouncing it.

"It's called an aquarium. Your daddy and your mama took you when you were younger. You remember that?"

Polly looked up at her and nodded her head, her eyes troubled. "Right, I almost forgot."

"It was several years ago." It had been the year her mother died. Polly had barely been three, so it was a wonder she remembered much about it.

"Aunt Summer, I'm glad you came here to watch me. And I've been thinking. I heard you talking about going out on that boat with Jonah. When me and Mama would go in the boat, we had so much fun. I mean, before she drowned. She loved that boat. I don't know what happened that time when she hit those rocks and I got thrown in the water and she hit her head and left me, but I was thinking, she really liked that water. And I was thinking maybe I could go on that boat with you and Jonah next time."

Summer's heart tugged tight and ached with the pain she still hadn't gotten used to. She had loved her sister-in-law and she had hated so badly for her little niece to lose her mother.

"If you think you want to go out on the water, I think you're very much capable of going out there with us. We'll ask your daddy and then I'll see if Jonah will take us. He knows where the dolphins are and the sea turtles. You're going to love it."

Summer thought about Jonah and she knew that other than Hunter taking his daughter out on the water,

Jonah was the perfect person. "Do you want your daddy to come too?"

"Daddy still gets really sad. We can ask him but he doesn't have to go because I think Jonah will be really good at it. He has a lot of boats, doesn't he?"

"Yes, honey, he does. And I think you're very right—you would be very safe with Jonah. We'll ask your daddy and let him decide what he wants to do."

* * *

Summer took Polly for muffins at Bake My Day to celebrate seeing the manatee. They had dropped in once before and the muffins were to die for but they hadn't been back. It was tempting to make a stop every day because the muffins were so good but Summer feared that they would start showing up on her hips if they came too often. Although Rosie kept telling her she had the sugar-free kind made with monk fruit and they were delicious, so today she planned to try one of those. She crossed her fingers that it would be as good as the ones made with real sugar. Rosie even made some with coconut flour and almond flour so that it was friendly to those who couldn't eat regular flour. She might have to try that too.

The thing was, Rosie Sinclair was a genius when it came to muffins. She had muffins that had some of the strangest names but they were fantastic, not that Summer had tried all of them. But Rosie had this little platter on top of the counter with little pieces of muffins cut up so customers could test as many as they wanted. She had to admit that she had tested almost all of them. But her favorite was the lemon poppy seed with cream cheese filling. She had heard that a lot of people liked the one with orange marmalade and cinnamon, and then there were a few who she had seen who just proclaimed that the strawberry with cream cheese was the most amazing of all.

Summer had this thing for lemon, though, so, as they were standing there with Rosie grinning at her from the other side of the counter, she couldn't help herself. "I'll have to have another one of those lemon poppy seed muffins. It's just fabulous."

Rosie chuckled. "I try to make them so that people

can't resist them. I have a great job." She grinned happily then focused on Polly, who was studying the glass cabinet with a serious expression on her face. "Young lady, have you figured out which one of those you want?"

"Well, I see that Rainbow Delight. Isn't that what you called that one the other day while I was in here? The sprinkle-covered one?"

"You remembered. Yes, that is it. Is that the one you want?"

"I think so. But if it's okay with my aunt, I'd also like one of those chocolate ones too. It looks scrumptious."

Scrumptious. Summer almost laughed out loud.

Rosie smiled too. "And coffee for you, Summer, and juice for you, Polly?"

"Yes, juice, and I'll take an Americano if you have it, with creamer, please," Summer agreed.

"A tall blonde Americano." Rosie smiled at her. "It can work for brunettes too."

"Well, I hope so because that's the one I like."

Rosie went to get their order.

Gigi, who worked at the bakery, was wiping off a table. "I hear you went on a boat ride with Jonah the other day."

"I didn't. But I'm going to," Polly answered first.

Summer clarified, "It was great. The water is so pretty. And Jonah was very kind to invite me to go on a boat ride."

"He has always been the nicest guy," Gigi said. "I went to school with him. He was a heartbreaker and never even realized it."

Summer could well imagine all the girls who probably had huge crushes on him during school. And afterward.

Rosie set the muffins on the counter. "He's a sweetie, but so is my Adam."

"Yes, he is, and always was," Gigi assured her. "Adam was just always focused on becoming a doctor. He and Tate were total opposites."

"And good-looking too, don't you think?"

Here we go, she thought. "Yes, he is very good-looking but I think the kindness of him is the main attraction, don't you?"

Rosie studied her. "I agree, but his looks don't hurt anything."

Polly stared at them. "I think he is handsome, like my daddy. And I think he's super nice because he's going to take me out on the boat. I haven't been out on a boat in a long time and my daddy said that if he can't go with us whenever Jonah sets up the boat ride that it's okay if I go out there with Jonah and my Aunt Summer."

"Well, I think that you'd be quite safe with those two." Rosie set their order on the counter just as the doors opened and Lila, Doreen, Birdie, and Mami hustled inside.

"Well, what do we have here?" Mami's big, hot-pink caftan flowed around her as she walked toward little Polly. "This little cutie must be getting her a muffin and a juice."

Polly looked at her in amazement. "I am. How did you know?"

Summer looked at the muffin and juice sitting on the counter and smiled to herself.

Mami grinned. "I know things. I know that little

girls like yourself like rainbow muffins and orange juice."

Polly cocked her head to the side. "You're a very smart lady. And I like your dress. It's like a big ole kite and I like to fly kites. Does it ever lift you up in the air like maybe you're going to fly away when there's a big wind blowing?"

That got laughs from everybody. Mami especially, considering Mami was not a small person. "Well, honey, it might take a hurricane to lift me up in the air but you know, that might be fun. I went parasailing one time—not in this dress, mind you—and I was a little bit younger when I did it. But it was really fun being up there, way high up above the water, floating underneath that parachute. Yes, I liked it a lot, come to think of it." She looked at her friends who stood behind her, smiling. It was odd that they hadn't interjected yet, but then again, they hadn't had a chance. "Any of you girls up for going and finding a place we can go parasailing? This little gal just got me thinking about that and I think it might be fun for us to take a little ride up in the sky."

Little bitty Birdie grunted, "I am not gettin' pulled up into the air with my feet dangling down like shark bait. Have you lost your mind?"

Doreen frowned. "Count me out. With these boobs—oh excuse me—" She covered her mouth and glanced down at Polly, then whispered, "I'd likely flip upside down and bring the whole lot of us down and I'd drown."

Mami grimaced, looking at Doreen's chest. "You do have a point. Lila, it's just you and me."

Lila didn't look convinced. "Mami, I don't know if you should get in a parasail either."

Mami frowned. "Are you implying it wouldn't hold me up? Because it's made for two people." She harrumphed. "I've seen big men get up there in those things. Don't be talking about my body size. Just because I'm a few pounds and about a yardstick taller than you doesn't mean I can't parasail."

Birdie grinned. "I'm gonna take y'all's picture up there. Go for it, Lila."

Lila frowned. "I was just saying you are really tall and you're really broad. And I'm a chicken, and not ashamed of it. I'm not getting my feet off the sandy ground out there on that beach. Plus, I tend to agree with Birdie. If I was up there, I'd probably just find me a shark below me and I'm not comfortable with that little rope keeping me out of harm's way. I like a little something more solid between me and a shark."

The room laughed.

Mami just shook her head. "I'm the leader of a bunch of Chicken Littles. Where is your sense of adventure?"

"Well," Lila said as Doreen bit her lip and Birdie grinned, unashamed. "Better to be a chicken than shark bait. Right, Birdie?"

"Exactly."

Polly frowned up at them. "I don't know if I want to get in a boat if I have to worry about being shark food. Sharks don't look nice."

Mami looked mortified, as did the others.

"Oh, honey," she crooned. "I didn't mean to scare you about a shark. If you're in a boat, you don't have anything to worry about. It would take a mighty big shark to get a boat to sink. Besides, we have never had a shark attack here. Please, don't let my *friends* upset you. Let's talk about your muffins. Rosie, I'm going to have a rainbow muffin like this cutie pie. And then maybe y'all can come over here and sit down with us. We haven't had a chance to visit since you moved into town." She eyed Summer with a smile.

Summer got the strangest feeling that she was about to get interrogated.

Lila stepped up to the counter. "Rosie, my regular, please—strawberry cream cheese delight. I hear your husband and his brothers are going to be in the regatta this year. That's going to be fun, to watch the Sinclair brothers compete in the annual sailboat competition again."

"It certainly is," Doreen said. "That used to be a tradition. Until they grew up."

"Yes, ma'am, that's what Adam tells me. He's looking forward to it. Although, I've never actually been on a sailboat. I think we're all going to go out on one soon and they're going to let us all ride and experience it. I can't wait. It sounds like it's a lot of fun. The whole town gets involved, so I guess it's going to be an excuse for another festival?"

Mami grinned. "Of course it is. We *love* festivals. Any excuse to get everyone together and bring the tourists out. But this particular event brings in a lot of people, you know. "

Lila looked intently at Rosie. "You're going to have to hire people to sell muffins and you're going to have to come down and watch the race because with your husband being involved, you'll want to see it."

Rosie grinned. "Yes, ma'am, that's my plan. Gigi said she's going to work and I'm bringing in my other two girls, too—my temps are going to come work, too. And I'm going to take the day off. It's going to be so fun. You'll have to come too, Summer."

"Yes, you will," Mami said.

They all headed across the room to a table by the window.

Lila sat and patted a chair for them. "This is going to be fun. You know we don't get to visit with little girls that often."

Summer wanted to take the focus off her and Polly. She smiled and sank into the seat. "So tell me about this race," she said. "You've been having it for a long time, it seems like."

Birdie took a drink of her black coffee and set it down. "Yup, our founding fathers started this race a long time ago and there were a few families in town who took it to heart. They've had feuds over this race but it seems like the feuds have died down. Pretty much most of the kids of the ones who were feuding moved away and now it's just a fun little race with friendly competition."

"And we sure enjoy it." Birdie grinned then took a swig of coffee.

Mami continued, "The Sinclair boys beat everyone when they were in school. When you've got four strong boys all about the same age who were born to sail, it's hard to beat. They think on the same level, you know what I mean…it's almost like they think for each other when they're out there. But it's been awhile so they could be rusty."

Doreen looked at her with a shocked expression. "I bet they're not. Those boys were born knowing what to do. I bet it comes right back to them, just like riding a bicycle. Plus, you know they're going to start practicing. I think they're practicing this evening…I think I heard that somewhere."

That perked Summer up. "Where do they practice at?" she asked, casually.

Birdie hitched her head toward the wall that faced the docks. "Right out there in the bay."

"And if you can't see it there, Duke's, the sports bar down the way, always puts it on the television. It's not televised but they have a closed circuit camera set up on the top of the building that they film it with and show it on the big screen. Me, I like to sit out there on the dock and watch it."

"I do too," Lila said. "We all bring our binoculars."

They talked about the race a little bit more.

When Polly finished her muffin and her juice, she looked up at Summer. "Do you think that while we're here, we can walk down to the dock and see when Jonah can take us out on the boat?"

Summer hadn't planned to let herself go close to the dock anytime soon. But with Polly looking up at her like that and all the ladies looking at her expectantly, she wasn't sure what she should do.

Lila patted her on the shoulder. "Honey, that is a great idea. You two should go down there. He's always at that dock. He lives there, you know. If he's not outside, just go inside and you'll find him. He's got a great business down there. I just love going down there."

What could she say? "Okay, Polly, then I think we'll do that. You ready to go?"

Polly grinned and shot out of her chair. "Yes. I'm going to go see if I can get me a boat ride. I love to boat ride. My mama used to take me boat riding but she died in the water and I haven't done it...since me and her had our accident. But I'm ready to do it now."

Summer closed her eyes and let her heartache take over for a minute. When she opened her eyes, all the ladies were looking at her with stunned expressions.

"We are so sorry," Lila said.

"So very, very sorry," Mami crooned, tears in her eyes. "You are a very brave young girl."

Birdie coughed, and Summer suspected the gruff

older lady was also fighting tears. "What happened? It's so sad, poor dear."

Doreen dabbed at her eyes and couldn't speak.

Rosie and Gigi had heard, too, and looked as stunned as the older ladies.

"There was an accident. I didn't mention it before but, yes, a few years ago, before we moved here, there was an accident. Polly and her mama were in a boat and it wrecked. Polly's mother…she drowned. Polly was wearing her life vest and they got her out of the water. And she's starting to do really well and I think she's a very brave girl because she wants to go back in the water."

Everyone agreed she was brave as they dabbed at their eyes.

Mami reached out and gave Polly a big hug. "Darling, I think you're the bravest little girl I've ever met. And your mama—she would be so proud of you. Now, you go out there and let Jonah set a time to go on the boat. He really does know what he's doing. And safety first—you always wear your life vest. And I'm so sorry about your little mama."

Polly sniffed. "Thank you. I like to tell people about my mama because I like to talk about her. Now I can talk about her with y'all."

They all said *Yes, you can* simultaneously.

When they left, Summer felt relieved. Sometimes being new in a town was hard because you just didn't know what you were going to get asked or who you were going to meet, who was going to be the kind of person you could trust with things of the heart like that. But she felt really good about everyone she met inside the bakery.

And it was like Jonah said: if she could bring herself to tell people about her problem like Polly just told them her problem, then she could only imagine how they would rally around her, just like they did with Polly.

Even her counselor encouraged her at her recent meeting, to bring more friends into her circle of support. But she just wasn't ready.

CHAPTER TEN

Jonah was coming out of his office when he spotted Summer and Polly coming through the big open doors at the end of the bay. His pulse picked up and he was instantly having a better day. He had been dealing with a warranty over a boat and it hadn't been going his way. But Summer and her beautiful smile made everything okay. He really wondered about how quickly he had become attached to this beautiful woman. It was shocking, actually, but there was no denying it.

"Hello, ladies. You just brightened my day. What

are y'all out and about doing?"

Polly giggled. "We came to see you. My daddy said that he has to work for another week and a half and since I really want to go on a boat ride, he said that if you can take me before he gets off that he would trust me going out with you, but if you don't have time then we can wait until he gets home and then we can all go."

Jonah looked at Summer for clarification. *Was Hunter really going to let him take his daughter out when she hadn't been on a boat in all this time?* Summer looked a little bit cautious, like he was. "Well, I guess if that's what your Aunt Summer and your daddy want, then I'm good to take you out. You're going to come, too, right?"

She nodded. "Yes. Hunter thinks that if Polly is ready that he doesn't want to do anything to hold her back. And believe me, she's been hounding us both about this. She wants to go."

He looked at Polly and she smiled at him. The little girl was like an angel. She had dark curls and big eyes that won his heart every time she looked at him.

He could only imagine the pain she felt. And he wondered how long it had taken her to decide that she wanted to get back in the water. And why was her daddy not making sure he was the one to take her? The thoughts puzzled him. Unless Hunter hadn't been completely truthful and there might be some reason he didn't want to get back in the water.

"Well, I can't go today. We're practicing this evening for the sailboat race me and my brothers are in. And we're practicing again tomorrow and I've got meetings and a boat I have to look at tomorrow. So, two days—day after tomorrow…how would that work?"

Polly jumped up and clapped her hands and then wrapped her arms around his legs and hugged him. "It would be great. It would just be great. Thank you."

He looked at Summer for answers to his unspoken questions; she shrugged and closed her eyes momentarily and looked back at him with questions of her own in her eyes.

As part of Hunter's duties at the fire department, he—like most in the department—stayed there during his shift. Until Brad had met Lulu, his brother had spent more than half his time sleeping at the fire department. It was good they had more help now; it would give some of them more time off.

But because Hunter was working, that meant Jonah couldn't get as many answers from Summer as he wanted unless he could figure out a way to get Polly out of earshot for a little while. Hopefully playing in a boat would help give him the time he needed.

Jonah showed Polly one of his bigger boats. She looked up at it with her big eyes and grinned at him. "That's a really big boat. Is that the one we're going to go out on? Because it looks really safe."

"Yes, it is very safe, and I'll see if we can take that one out. You want to get up there and look at it? Here, I'll put you up there and you can pretend like you're driving."

"Sure, that'd be great. I need to learn how to drive a boat."

He lifted the little girl up into the boat and watched her as she went directly to the platform and climbed up the steps, going over to the boat controls.

She sat in the big comfortable seat and looked as if she would be happy there for a while.

He turned to Summer, who was watching him. "What's the deal about Hunter not wanting to take his daughter out on a boat after it being her first time since her mom died? It seems really odd. I'm figuring there's more to the story."

She glanced at Polly, who was still busy, and then she sighed. "She doesn't really want him to take her out. Subconsciously, we don't think she does. She has nightmares at night. I have nightmares at night. Her and I together…we're just a real mess. But Polly doesn't really remember her nightmares. She wakes up crying. But…Jonah, she has a type of amnesia where she doesn't really remember it all. So, I have to warn you that when we take her out, she could have an episode. It wouldn't be exactly like mine but she could remember something that upsets her. I didn't mean to be presumptuous but I truly feel like you're comfortable with that."

He felt pleased that she put such trust in him. He figured he was doing something right if she thought that about him. Gave him a lot to live up to. "I'm glad you feel that way. But about these nightmares…what happens in the nightmares to make you think she doesn't want her daddy to be on the boat?"

"Because in her nightmares, she's crying for her daddy to not get on the boat because he's going to die. Just like her mama. And she's almost hysterical."

Jonah's heart sank. "Poor kid. Poor Hunter. What a horrible mess."

"Exactly. He feels torn. He wants to get on the boat with her but also he doesn't want to get on the boat and then have her start having that nightmare. He just doesn't think that's good for her right now and the psychologist doesn't either. We talked about it and he's going to come talk to you. I was just going to tell him when we set the boat ride up and he's going to come tell you everything. He just hasn't had time yet. So if you end up having time to go by the firehouse, that would be great. But he thinks, and I agree, that if she goes by herself and everything is great then that could ease something inside her and then maybe she could transition into him getting on the boat with her.

If her nightmares were to hopefully subside some because she's facing a fear, I'd be so proud of her. She wants to do this. It's almost like something's driving her to get on a boat. She's been a little bit obsessed with it lately. Would you be willing to do this?"

"Absolutely. If it will help that little girl, then I'm up for anything. And I'll do whatever it takes to help you, too—remember that. What both of you have been through just hurts me."

She looked so sweetly at him and his heart turned over.

"Jonah Sinclair, you're a very good man. I just wanted to tell you that."

He really wanted to wrap his arms around her, hold her close, and tell her she was a really good person. But he didn't. He just had to satisfy himself by staring into those beautiful eyes of hers. "I think for you to call me that is an honor. Now, in a few minutes, I'm going to meet my brothers out there and we're going to get on a boat and sail. You'll be able to see us doing some maneuvers out there from the pier, if you and Polly want to watch a little bit. Maybe one day, not yet, but one day we'll take her out on a sailboat. I think that right now maybe a boat with a bunch of engines might be better for her because it's got those high sides and might feel safer for her. I don't know—that's just my opinion."

"I think you're right. She and her mom were on a smaller boat when the accident happened. I think starting out with a big boat might be the best thing. And we might come watch the famous Sinclair brothers maneuver a sailboat for a little while."

He laughed. "What?"

"Oh, as if you didn't know you four Sinclairs are a legend from back when you sailed together every year. You are the talk of the town."

"Lila and her gals."

"Told us all about it. They were very sad when your brothers left town and broke up the team."

"Life moves and shifts. And now they're all back, except Tate. You met my brother Tate. He's flown in but he won't be here long, just long enough for this race—maybe two weeks. We're blessed we even get him for two weeks. He's a busy man—does all kinds of crazy stunts. He's a stunt man in Hollywood. He films documentaries. He shoots commercials, falling out of airplanes—he's all over the place. I can't keep up with him. But he's here right now and we're going to have fun. He gets to come home for a couple of days every once in a while and he enjoys coming when we're having festivals and hanging out with the whole family. My sister's going to be here but she's not going to get here until the actual race. She's almost as bad as him—she flies all over the place and takes pictures of dangerous spots and beautiful places. Her work is really sought-after. I think it all started with taking a wedding photo. World's crazy sometimes, you know."

Summer watched him. "And you stayed here. Very content, I think."

He had been, to a point. But now, he yearned for someone to share his life with. "I think sometimes people think I might be a little boring. I'm predictable but it's what I like. I like it here. I like having a stable business. I like building a nice retirement for a family I hope to have one day. Is it weird for a man to dream of picket fences and a wonderful wife?" He hesitated, then said what was on his heart. "Lately, those dreams had started to diminish. I'd become disillusioned, but suddenly, I'm starting to see that picket fence again."

He wasn't sure she would get what he was saying or whether it would scare her away. But the truth was out there now, whether she got it or not. He didn't break his gaze from hers when he said it.

Her eyes crinkled at the edges. "I think that anybody you imagined inside that picket fence with you should feel honored. And I hope you find her one day."

His lips lifted. He was patient; he would stand by her side and do everything he could to help her get her life back to the way it had been before she'd been attacked. "Thanks. Polly, are you ready to watch a sailboat race?"

Polly whirled around from where she'd been pretending to drive the boat. "Sure." She came to the edge; he reached up and took her by the arms, then lifted her out of the boat.

He set her on her feet. "Well then, let's head out. But don't you forget—we have a date for a boat ride."

She beamed at him. "I can't wait."

"I can't either." Summer smiled at him.

His heart stumbled with an emotion so strong it had his head spinning. "We're going to have a great time," he said. He hoped the days flew, the quicker the better so he could see Summer again.

CHAPTER ELEVEN

By the time Jonah and his brothers had spent the evening sailing, they'd felt as if they were in their youth again. Even with all of them in their thirties, this was a great reminder of how they had once been growing up. They had always had one another's backs and that was one reason they worked so well together during the race. Their dad always had them work together and they were used to doing things as a team. But being out on the boat, laughing and running that sailboat together, was fun. Jonah was glad that Adam had come home and taken the position as the physician in town. Brad had always been in Sunset Bay, like he'd been. They both liked living in this small town and always had. Tate was a different story. He would never slow down, and came home only briefly when he could. But as far as Jonah knew, Tate was happy with his career and not looking to settle down.

Jonah couldn't help glancing toward the shore to see whether the two cute dark brunettes were still sitting on the pier watching them but they weren't. Disappointment swept through him. He knew it was getting late and Polly probably had a bedtime schedule.

A few minutes later after they'd docked. he looked over at Tate. "Before we call it a night, tell us what your next move it."

Tate took a sip of his drink, laid one muscled arm across the back of his seat, and looked thoughtful. "I don't know. I'm finishing up a stunt job the week after I get back. Not sure what I'm going to do after that. I haven't lined up another movie just yet. I actually told my agent to send me a job over the next month only if it's an A-lister. I'm feeling itchy. I think it's time for me to go on an adventure. I don't do restless well."

Brad grinned at him. "Are you getting tired of being stuck on a movie set with all those beautiful women and impressing them by falling out of airplanes and off cliffs?"

"Or getting blown up and all that cool stuff?" Jonah asked.

Adam grinned. "Leave him alone. Someone has to do it."

They all chuckled, except Tate.

His brows creased. "Honestly, my body needs a break from everything I put it through. And as far as women on the set, yeah, there's a lot of gorgeous women on movie sets, but I'm looking at you two." He looked at Adam and Brad. "I'm seeing what you two have with Rosie and Lulu and it's making me think…about things I've never thought about. I thought thinking about settling down was at least a decade away, but it's hit me recently that I'm thirty-four years old. Ten years means forty-four."

Jonah was shocked that Tate was thinking a lot like he was. He was thirty-two and ready. He'd been ready but the right woman hadn't come along.

"What about you, Jonah? Are our brothers making you think about altering your life?"

"Big time. None of us are getting any younger. I never wanted to be in my forties or fifties, fathering babies. I want them in this decade. Better yet, within the next five years. The way we've been going, I totally understand why Mom was getting vocal about all of us being single."

Adam nodded. "Me, too. We're going to check next week to find out whether we're going to have a baby. That's a secret, though."

They all looked at Adam.

"Seriously?" Jonah was the first to ask.

Adam held up his hands. "Seriously. We really hope that it happens soon."

Brad nodded, smiling wistfully. "Us, too. Lulu said before we got married that she was ready to have babies now. And I mean, why wait? I love her and we waited a long time to find each other, so it's just a natural progression. And Hunter, our new fireman, has the cutest little girl. Makes me think about a child of my own every time I see Polly."

Tate looked at Jonah. "That's the little girl and her aunt who were with you earlier?"

"Yes. She is adorable."

Brad turned serious. "Hunter told me that he's going to let you take Polly out on a boat for the first time since her mom was killed in a boating accident."

Jonah frowned. "You knew about the accident?"

"Yeah, but he's not talked about it to many people. He said it wasn't a secret but he just wasn't talking about it a lot."

"I see. Yeah, we set the time today. Summer filled me in on her earlier today. She has nightmares over the terrible accident with her and her mom. If me taking her on a boat ride will help Polly get past the nightmares, then I'm up for that. She's a brave little girl."

Tate leaned forward, his elbows on his knees. "What's going on? What happened?"

Adam didn't look surprised at all and it hit Jonah that Hunter had probably already gone by and talked to him, too, considering he was the doctor in town. In case Polly needed Adam, he would be in on what her problems were.

"Polly and her mom were in a boat accident. Polly's five, I think—something like that—she's a little thing. Her mom wasn't wearing a life vest when the boat ran into some rocks and they were thrown from the boat. She drowned. Polly had on her life vest and it saved her. She still suffers from nightmares and she doesn't remember everything. It's been about two or three years now."

"That's terrible. Where was her dad?" Tate asked. "And he isn't going to be on the boat the first time she goes out on the water since the accident?"

"Summer said she has nightmares about him getting killed too, but that she's unaware of what she says during the nightmares. He doesn't want to trigger anything by being on the boat with her when she goes out the first time. It makes sense to me."

"Me too," Adam said, thoughtfully.

"It's a lot of responsibility," Jonah said, feeling the weight of it.

Tate met him with a hard, serious stare. "Jonah, if

anybody would be the one to choose, it would be you. I mean, you've got the heart of a lion and sensitivity of a teddy bear. And you're smart. You know boats and you know that water out there better than anyone. You're a very logical person to pick. But, if you didn't have that teddy bear personality and that heart you've got, you might not be. I mean, some gruff old dude who was good on boats wouldn't be right, no matter what. I see why they're asking you."

"He's right," Brad agreed. "I hope she doesn't have any kind of episode while she's out there but you know CPR and all kinds of emergency procedures. You'll be all right. Why don't you come by the firehouse tomorrow and talk to Hunter? He knew we were practicing today; he was going to run by and try to see you for a few minutes during his break. I know he wants to talk to you now that you all have a date."

He looked at Adam. "Yeah, Brad, I'll come by. Adam, do you have any advice for me? You're awful quiet over there. I have a feeling you know everything going on with Polly."

He nodded. "I do, but unlike you three who can sit

there and talk about it, I can't. Doctor-patient confidentiality, you know. But I'll say this—I agree with my brothers one hundred percent and I think it will be okay or I would suggest it not happening. There are different forms of amnesia. Sometimes it takes confronting something before the injured party can fully heal from it. I think that's what we're all hoping for. Be ready for any signs of her being really upset. Be ready to head back in if you need to. We don't need to push her, you know what I mean?"

"Yeah, I know what you mean and I'll take my time. Summer and I both will be watching. We will be very alert."

Brad stood and yawned. "Okay, well, guys, I, for one, think today was a success. I guess we will do it again tomorrow night unless I have a fire and I can't get here. I better head on back to the firehouse." He stepped off the boat and onto the pier. "Later, brothers," he said, heading down the long wooden pier lined with boats.

They all decided it was time to head in. He and his brothers secured the boat then said goodnight. Jonah headed up the stairs to his second-story apartment and went inside. He fixed a cup of coffee and then stood at the big picture windows overlooking the bay. The view was amazing but his thoughts weren't on the view, but on Summer and what she had been through and what Polly had been through. He hoped with all his heart that his brothers were right and he was the right person for this very delicate job for the precious cargo he would be carrying on the boat ride.

Because the weight of the responsibility of what he was going to do was heavy. And it was not something he could mess up.

This was one boat charter that had to be perfect.

* * *

The next morning, before six a.m., there was a knock on Jonah's apartment door. He had just gotten his clothes on after getting out of the shower. He was tugging his shirt down over his abs when he pulled the door open to find Hunter on the stoop.

Relieved to see Polly's daddy, Jonah pulled the

door wide. "Hunter, come in. I'm glad you came by. I planned to come see you this morning."

Hunter walked in, pausing just inside the door with his hands on his hips. "Summer told me last night that you had agreed to take Polly out. I knew I couldn't put it off any longer."

That struck Jonah as an odd statement. "Maybe we need to sit down and talk." He headed over toward the bay window and sank down in one of the chairs that overlooked the bay.

Hunter took the next one. "This is a great place. I'd never dreamed it was up here."

"Yeah, I've been single a long time and when I had to build this building, I just had them build me an apartment. I couldn't let the view go unused."

"I see why. Look, I can't thank you enough for agreeing to take my baby out on that boat."

He seemed nervous to Jonah. "I'll take good care of her but I needed to hear it from you that you were okay with this."

Hunter clasped his hands together and turned his serious eyes to Jonah. "The day my wife slammed that boat into the rocks was the most horrible day of my life. We had argued, terribly. She had told me she was leaving me, and I was blindsided. Completely. She was upset. I was upset. And we said some things I regret. She would regret them, too, if she'd had time to truly regret them. The accident happened two hours after our fight. She had scheduled to take the boat out. She was a fisherman. She loved it; she fished all the time. She was practically a professional—she won tournaments all the time. She knew how to run a boat. And Polly went with her a lot, so there wasn't any reason to think there was any danger, even though we had the fight.

"We had agreed to talk later. I had to go to the firehouse. My shift was starting and they were short-handed and, well, she was highly upset. I thought maybe some time to cool off would be a good thing. Little did I know I'd never see her again. It was surreal. The thing is, she knew boats; she knew the water. I still can't figure out how she ran that boat up on that rock like she did. I refuse to believe that it was on purpose."

"That's horrible. I am so sorry," Jonah said, not

even able to fathom what Hunter must be feeling. He had a lot of questions but he wasn't going to ask anything.

Hunter heaved in a sigh and sat up straight. "I've gone over it and over it in my mind and it had to have been an accident. She wouldn't have done anything to jeopardize Polly. All I can think of is there's something that happened that caused her to have that accident, unless she was so distracted by all the things she was thinking about. She loved Polly. I just can't imagine that she would've done anything to endanger our child." Hunter raked his hands through his hair, pausing to rub his temples.

Jonah waited, wondering why Summer hadn't told him this part.

As if hearing Jonah's thoughts, Hunter placed his hands on his knees and sighed. "Summer didn't want to go into all this with you. She felt like I needed to be the one to tell you. I believe that something happened that caused the accident and that Polly doesn't remember it. The doctors agree that she could have suppressed the memory. All I know is, some nights—

thank God, there are fewer than before—but some nights she wakes up, almost like she's in a trance and she's hysterical that I'm going to get into the water and that it's going to happen to me too. Now I'm afraid to get in the boat or the water with her. I'm very grateful to you. I talked to your brother Adam and he said that you're the best out there and that if she were to have a problem, you would get her back in. And he's going to be on call, also, if he's needed. Is that okay with you?"

Wow, he hadn't thought about all the scenarios of what could go down out there. "I'm good with it, but I'm not as positive about me being the right person as you seem to think. Adam is just as good on the water as I am and he's a trauma doctor. He's seen everything that could be seen in his line of work. He's been a trauma doctor in the busiest emergency rooms and trauma units in this country. Maybe she needs to build a relationship with Adam and he needs to take her out."

Hunter looked conflicted. "She's already latched on to you. She wants you. Whatever's driving her to do this, it started when she met you. I don't know why but you're the one she's picked for this very important boat trip."

Jonah had never in his life come up against anything like this. That little girl had walked up to him that day with her ice cream cone in hand and she had started the conversation. For some reason, she had chosen him and he didn't plan to let her down. He nodded. "All right, I'm in. We're going to do this. And we're going to go wherever she leads. But I promise you, we'll be back on this dock safe and sound tomorrow evening."

"You don't know how much this means to me. There's nothing like worrying about your child's well-being. And after what she went through, it's just a lot on my mind. I moved here because we needed a new beginning. I had no idea she was going to want to do this. But we're going with it and we're going to hope that when it's all over, she's going to come out healthier. She is a delight, don't you think?"

"She is that. She's special."

"I think so. And Jonah, you are too. Summer tells me how you are with her, that you're good with her, and it means a lot. I wouldn't trust her to just anybody."

Jonah gave him a smile, feeling humble. "Hunter, can I ask you about Summer?"

Hunter nodded, almost looking relieved that they were moving on to something different.

"How is she doing, really?" Jonah watched Hunter's lips flatten into a grim line.

"Summer is strong. My sister is going to come through what happened to her. Even if the guy had ended up raping her, she would've made it through. She's a fighter but she lost a part of herself that day. She's fighting really hard to get it back. Seems like you have attracted all the women in my life. It's hard to believe they are both having such problems right now. I don't want to put any pressure on you, man, but you've got two very special people who seem to trust you. And that's a very precious thing."

"Believe me, just between you and me, I really like your sister. So of course, I'm taking this very seriously. Are they sure this guy is going to be in prison for a long time?"

"Yeah, I don't think he's getting out. They're finding more and more against him every day. He is a bad dude. With luck, there will be enough evidence against him she won't have to show up in court to testify against him in a month. Summer is determined to face her fears in that courtroom if she has to. And to tell you the truth, if they tell her she can't go or isn't needed, I think she might go anyway. Sometimes I think she tries to be stronger than she needs to be."

"Well, the way I look at it, we just need to support her and help her be as strong as she can be on that day."

For the first time since he had walked through his door, Hunter smiled. "I agree. And, Jonah, thank you again. You need anything, you holler. We'll all be waiting tomorrow on standby if you need us."

After Hunter left, Jonah stood at his window. He placed his arms on the thick steel beams that housed all the glass in architectural rows; he dropped his head to look at the floor and said a prayer.

CHAPTER TWELVE

The sun was shining when Summer and Polly walked down the docks of the marina toward the huge, gorgeous boat that Jonah stood on, waving at them. Polly clapped her hands. "Look, Aunt Summer! Look at it! It's huge! It's beautiful! And…Jonah—hey, Jonah!" She jumped up and down and then started running.

Summer grabbed her shirt collar. "Hold on there, little girl." She chuckled. "You need to stay with me. We don't need you falling into the water because you're so excited."

"But I am excited! Come on, you run with me."

"We're not running. We're going to get there in just a second."

Sure enough, fifteen steps later, they came up to the boat, with Jonah climbing out of the boat to stand on the dock. He had his hands on his hips and he was grinning. The man was so handsome that her heart fluttered in her chest. She was really shocking herself about how much she was thinking of him. She'd come here to get over what had happened to her, true, but she hadn't even dreamed that she would be contemplating dating again. But she was.

"How are the two most beautiful ladies in the world doing this morning?"

Polly giggled. "I'm a girl. My aunt is beautiful, isn't she?"

Summer looked at her niece, shocked that she would be trying to get Jonah to tell her that she was beautiful. "What are you up to, little girl?"

Polly giggled again. "You are beautiful, Aunt Summer. I always think so."

"She's right, you know. You are beautiful," Jonah said. "And you, young lady, are beautiful too. And we're going to have a fantastic day out on the water today. I have it all planned out." Then he leaned down and whispered, "I took your aunt to a very secret place when we went on our boat ride and there's all kinds of dolphins that hang out there and usually stingrays and sea turtles. There's a little dock if you want to fish. Do you like to fish?"

"I do like to fish. Do you know my mama was a wonderful fisherwoman? She could catch anything."

Summer was in awe at how it was so natural for Polly to speak of her mother like that. She was so happy that the accident hadn't caused her to not talk about her mama. The only thing she didn't talk about were the moments leading up to the wreck and after the accident.

"I did hear that your mother was an excellent fisherwoman and I bet you take after her."

"I hope so. I'm going to try anyway. So take me there and let's see what I can do. Do you have a fishing pole my size?"

"Yes, in fact, I do. Although, you can use a big one if you want to. But I have a special one just for you. And I will be your hook baiter. You don't have to touch any of the bait if you don't want to."

"My mama said that if you are a real fisherperson or fisherwoman or fisherman, you have to touch the bait. So it's icky, but I can do it."

Summer grinned, enjoying the exchange.

By the look on Jonah's face, he was enjoying it too. "Your mama was a very smart woman. All right, are you ready to get on the vessel? Because, girl, this is a vessel—it is top of the line, all the way. Even has a bed downstairs in the cabin if you need to take a nap."

She looked at him with a scrunched-up face. "I am too old for naps. Ask Aunt Summer."

Summer watched their interplay. "Yes, she is."

"Okay, then we're ready to go and no naps for you. But, now, if I decided *I* need to take a nap, then you can take over and I'll go take one. Because it gets hot out there sometimes and a nap just feels good."

Polly giggled. "You don't really take a nap. Naps are for babies."

"Are you calling me a baby?"

Polly grinned and didn't say anything.

Jonah laughed. "No, I'm not going to take a nap, I promise. I'm not going to have anybody calling me a baby. I'm the captain of this ship. Let's get on board."

And with that, just like he had done when they visited him at his boat business, he lifted Polly up and placed her over the edge of the boat and into the boat. And then he hopped on board and held his hand out to Summer. "May I help you?"

She could have done it herself but she realized she would use any and all excuses to touch Jonah, so she slipped her hand in his and smiled. "Yes, you may." His hand closed over hers: strong, comforting, and sending thrills up and down her arm. She stepped into the boat and paused next to him as every cell in her body warmed. She felt so comfortable with him.

He said softly, "I think we're going to have a good day. She seems ready."

She smiled at him. "I think so. I'm glad we're with you."

* * *

The wind and the sun and the salt in the air just made for a great time. Jonah kept his eyes glued on the water around them but he frequently took in the expressions on Polly's and Summer's faces. Both seemed to be doing okay. He was nervous; he just tried not to show it. Summer gave him a grateful look and came to stand beside him. Polly sat in the seat, looking as if she knew exactly what she was doing on a boat. She didn't seem nervous at all and he found that a little bit strange given the last time she was on a boat.

Summer placed a hand on his arm and squeezed lightly. "Thank you. She just told me that she was liking this a lot. So where are we going to go first?"

He glanced at Polly, who was watching the water intently. He had told her to keep an eye out for dolphins and sea turtles. He hoped they would see a lot of them. He was heading toward where he knew a pod of porpoise liked to hang out. "I think we'll go to the island. If we don't see any porpoise or sea turtles along the way, then we'll do some fishing. I didn't show you the pier, you know—it's on the other side of the island, in the mangroves. There are little fish all over the place there. If she likes to fish because it was something to do with her mother—and I kind of think that she is wanting to do this because of her mother—then that might be a good thing. What do you think?"

"I think that's a fantastic idea. I'm curious about the little dock, too. I wonder why it's there?"

"A long time ago, someone owned that little island. I haven't researched it but somebody may still own it. But it's got a nice dock. It's aging but it's sturdy and there are all kinds of little fish that hang out down there. I've even seen little nerf sharks, which I think she would find exciting."

"Oh goodness, we had a big talk about sharks one day at Bake My Day with Mami and her friends. Polly was intrigued. She's been fishing with her mother a lot and there's no telling what they saw. But, for her age, I would think what would be at that dock will be something that she'd enjoy. As far as fishermen go, anytime you can catch a lot of little fish or any kind of fish, it's a good day, I think. I'll go back over there and sit with her but I just wanted to ask you that."

He wanted to cup her face and brush his lips across hers and ask her how she was doing. But they hadn't known each other that long; his feelings for her had just exploded and he had to force himself to go very slowly. She was tender and he didn't want to run her off or scare her. He wanted to help her. "Summer, anything you need, you just ask, okay?"

She looked both relieved and touched by his question. "Thank you."

He forced himself not to watch her go back to sit down with Polly and instead watched the water.

Along the way, Polly spotted the dolphins. And she jumped up from her seat and clapped her hands excitedly. "I see them," she exclaimed.

He slowed down and hoped that they swam near the boat. Hoped they gave the little girl a big show. And they did. Three of them swam to the boat and then swam around the boat; they jumped up out of the water and played. He would've sworn that they knew he had precious cargo on the boat who needed to see them. Polly was thrilled. Summer was also thrilled that her niece seemed to be handling everything so wonderfully. By the time the island came into view, he asked Polly whether she wanted to walk on the beach or fish on the pier.

She did not hesitate. "I want to fish. My mama always took me fishing. I want to catch a fish. It's been a long time since I caught a fish."

Jonah's heart squeezed. "Honey, you're going to catch a fish."

He pulled the boat around the small island, past the beach where the mangroves started showing up. The greenery stretched out along the far side of the beach. The little brown weathered pier, with its sturdy post, had been built by someone who knew what they were doing and had lasted for years. But as far as he knew, very seldom had someone been using it. It came into view; he pulled into the docking area, leaving the big boat on the outside of the dock poles as he tied it up.

"Okay, I'm going to get off first. I'm going to get all the bait buckets and the poles. I'll set them out here and then, after I do that, I'll help you ladies off the boat. Okay, Polly, you'll keep your life jacket on. Summer you will, too, and as you can tell, I'll keep mine on also."

He didn't always wear a life vest on the water—he was so used to the water—but because of what Polly had been through and the fact that her mother would probably be alive if she had her vest on, he wore his and he would continue to wear it. He had a light one that was fairly unobtrusive but automatically inflated if he were to fall in the water. Today, he wore a bulky, orange vest to visibly show Polly he was wearing a vest too. He would not want anything he did to trigger some unpleasant memory.

After he had everything out on the pier and ready, he lifted an excited little girl onto the pier and then helped Summer step out onto it. Then they walked toward the mangroves, about halfway along the pier where he had set the buckets.

Polly gasped in complete awe as she looked down

and saw small fish everywhere in the clear water.

* * *

Jonah baited plenty of hooks in the next hour, but he was surprised that Polly hadn't been kidding—she didn't mind baiting a hook. She just didn't bait it fast enough for all the fish she was catching. The kid would put the hook in the water and a little fish would instantly take the bait; she would haul it out, giggling and laughing. Summer would be laughing, too.

Summer looked at him, her eyes twinkling as he took a slippery fish off the hook. "This is perfect. She's going to catch as many fish as she wants today. I think it's so good for her. What do you think, Polly?"

"I'm having a blast. Even me and my mama never caught this many fish! How many fish have I caught so far?"

Jonah had been keeping up with how many fish they'd caught. Most of them they were releasing back into the water. "So far, fourteen." He smiled.

"*Fourteen*. Awesome."

He knew that this would be a good place. It didn't matter whether they had been big fish or not. For Polly, today was just about catching something and bringing back a part of her life that she had shared with her mother and had lost along with the loss of her mother.

They had been fishing for about forty-five minutes when Polly squealed and pointed into the water. "Is that a shark?"

"Yes, ma'am, it is. That's a little brown—well, they look brown in the water but it's actually a gray tone. See how much he looks like he's brown? That's because of the shades of the plant life down there with him." The water was only about four to ten feet deep along the pier. Everything down there was visible and the shark was hiding in the long tender strands of vegetation. It was only about three feet long and it was a nurse shark, which was what he thought would be here. He wouldn't ever take her around something dangerous, especially if there was even a small chance that she could fall off the pier. But to see one in its habitat was fun. "Have you ever been to an aquarium where they let you pet sharks?"

"Yes. I went once and I got to pet one."

"That's probably the kind you petted right there. They wouldn't put one in there that could come around and hurt you."

"They feel really weird. They're rough and then they're smooth."

"Yes, they are. It's like instead of having two moods, they have two feels on their skin."

"Exactly." Summer smiled at him.

He figured he would do just about anything for that smile.

After they had been there for about an hour and a half, he told them that they probably needed to pack up and head back.

"Okay. Are we going to eat a snack?" Polly asked.

"I was wondering when you were going to be hungry. I have all kinds of food for you. Once we get in the boat, we'll go down into the galley and we'll eat on the boat. How's that sound?"

"That sounds fun."

They packed up and got back on the boat. He

drove them around to where they could see the little beach. He had decided it would be better to eat on the boat today, to keep her on it as much as possible. He had packed a wonderful lunch; his mom had helped him figure out what a little kid might like to eat. They had peanut butter and jelly sandwiches, and some chicken salad sandwiches. He had chocolate chip cookies and snickerdoodle cookies, chips, and dips. He had gone a little bit overboard but he wanted to make sure she had a good time.

He sat on the side of the table that Summer was sitting on. Polly had the whole bench to herself across from them. She had all kinds of food spread out in front of her and took little bites of everything, just having a great time and chattering up a storm about all the fish she had caught. Summer's thigh touched his and he was very aware that she was next to him. And he hoped that today had helped her get even more comfortable with him.

When their hands brushed as they both reached for the salt, he glanced at her and she smiled at him. "You know that's not good for either one of us."

He grinned. "Depends on who you ask. Salt's natural—it's all that other junk that we eat that's not good for us, I think. It's one of those foods that there's question marks about, you know? And it sure is good."

"I know what you mean. I think I'll give sugar up before I give my salt up."

"I agree. Although, I was thinking that when we get back to the dock, we can walk down to the big pier and we can all get us an ice cream cone. How's that sound? Me, I can *always* eat ice cream."

"Me too, I think that sounds great." Polly grinned. "I can eat ice cream all the time. I don't have to have the salt but I like the ice cream."

Summer and Jonah laughed.

Polly got quiet. Looking thoughtful, she tilted her head to the side and stared at them. "Jonah, do you like my Aunt Summer?"

He almost choked on the chip he had just bit into. "Well, Polly, I do. There's a lot about your aunt to like. I like you, too."

"But I mean, do you like her like my daddy and my mama liked each other? They loved each other.

162

And I worry about my daddy. He misses my mama."

Jonah had a sinking sensation in his stomach. *Poor kid.* He met Summer's gaze. She looked very thoughtful.

She reached across the table and opened her hand. Polly laid hers in Summer's and the two stared at each other. "Sweetie, your daddy loved your mama very much. And he hurts on the inside, just like you do. But he's learning to move on and live without your sweet mama, too. And it's hard. I think that you are a very sweet girl to notice that. He's very happy he has you. And I can tell you that your mama is very happy that your daddy has you to help him smile. And to help him remember her. Because you like to talk about her and that's good because you know that helps him talk about her."

Polly's eyes suddenly teared up. "I don't want to forget my mama. But unless I look at her picture sometimes, I start not seeing her face in my mind. And sometimes I forget some of the things we did. That's why I wanted to go fishing today and ride on a boat because, it helped me remember her better. And that makes me happy. I hope Daddy will come on the boat."

Summer looked at Jonah and then she looked back at Polly. She was still holding her hand. She squeezed gently and he saw Polly squeeze Summer's hand too. Summer cleared her throat and he knew she was emotional—*he* was emotional.

"Baby, your daddy would love to take you on the boat. If you're okay with that. You've done really great today. We were worried you might have a hard time."

"I'm fine. I wasn't sure if I wanted Daddy to come but now I do. I think it will be fun for us to be on the boats again. And I love to fish."

"Then we'll tell your daddy that and I think he'll be so happy. He didn't come today just because he didn't want to make it hard on you. But he trusted Jonah with all of his heart and that's why he let Jonah take us."

"I know. I trust Jonah, too."

Jonah's radio crackled and he heard an alert. He got up. "Excuse me for a minute. I need to go check on that."

He left the cabin and went quickly up the stairs into the boat's dash controls, where he grabbed the mic so that he could quiet the sound inside the cabin. He didn't want the girls to hear what was going on.

"What's up?" He listened to the dispatchers and the alert was that there was a boat in trouble. *Man in water.* He immediately knew when he looked at the coordinates that he was closer than the other boats. He broke into the alert. "I'm on my way. We can get there before anyone."

CHAPTER THIRTEEN

Cutting fast through the water with huge motors in the large boat Jonah made it to the capsized boat within record time. The moment they spotted the boat, Polly started crying.

Summer held her close. "I'm so sorry you're having to see this, sweetie. But there's a man in the water somewhere out here and we've got to find him. Jonah has to find him and we have to try to save him. Do you understand?"

Polly sniffed. "There's a man in the water?"

Jonah had pulled his binoculars out and scanned

the water, hoping and praying that he could see the man. That the man had on a life jacket. "Yes, he's out here somewhere. If you spot him, let us know. If we all look together, maybe we'll find him and maybe we'll rescue him, just like you were rescued, Polly."

Polly stood and started looking too. Summer held her hand. "My mama and me were in the water. We have to find the man."

Jonah was scared about what this might do psychologically to Polly. He hadn't brought her out with the plans to try to rescue someone but he couldn't not try to find this man. Polly gripped the edge of the boat and then she and Summer came up into the passenger seat in the captain's deck and stood beside him. They all searched the water as he drove the boat slowly.

Jonah's heart was sinking and then suddenly Polly screamed. "I see him!"

He started in the direction she pointed. Sure enough, there in the distance was a man. And he was moving. Jonah cut the boat toward him and within moments, they pulled beside him and had him in the boat. He was bleeding from a gash on his head. Jonah immediately got him seated below deck. Summer put pressure on the wound with towels. Jonah called it in and Polly rode beside him as they raced toward the shore. He called Hunter and he called Brad. They were waiting on the dock when they got there.

They took over immediately, their paramedic skills useful as they worked on the man. Jonah was heartsick and completely worried about Polly. When they got the man fixed up and in the ambulance that took him to the hospital, Hunter had already looked at Polly to make sure she wasn't going into shock or anything. Jonah had been watching her very closely on the trip in to make sure of the same thing. But the kid seemed fine. He wasn't sure he would've been as fine as she was in her situation.

While Hunter was taking care of his daughter, Brad came over and clapped a hand on Jonah's back. "You did good, man. You okay? You look a little shell-shocked."

Jonah looked at his brother. "That wasn't how I had the day planned. It was a great day. That is one amazing kid right there. She just wanted to go fishing so she could remember her mom. Could you imagine? She was worried about forgetting her mom and fishing was the connection that she knew would help her. A kid knew that. And then that call came in. Brad, I didn't want to go but how do you not go try to save somebody when you're the closest boat to them?"

"Jonah, don't beat yourself up. You did what you had to do. And she seems like she's okay. I don't see signs that she's going into shock and her dad's got her now. And you and Summer did amazing. You started out with a lot on your plate with those two and it ended with even more—you did a great job. You got everybody stabilized; you kept everybody calm and you got that boat back here. Nobody could ask for anything more. And who knows—maybe what happened today will help Polly move on."

Jonah nodded. "I hope you're right."

Hunter came over. "Thank you, Jonah. You don't need to worry about anything. You did what you had to do. And Summer just whispered to me that you helped Polly when she was at first upset about the boat wreck.

That you calmed her and you talked to her about her mom. I don't know…maybe I need to talk to her more about her mom. Sandra was a great person. Yeah, it ended crazy weird between her and me, and I'll never know the whole of it but she was a good mom and I loved her. I guess for me that's why I'm so confused still. What happened just really screwed me up. But, for Polly, I'm going to have to start talking more about her mom and thinking less about the turmoil it brings me. Thank you. Well, I'm going to take Polly home. Brad, I know I'm still on shift but…"

"You go, man. We'll cover for you tonight. You need to be with your daughter," Brad said.

Jonah went over, knelt beside Polly and took her hands. "How's my brave girl?"

Polly wrapped her arms around his neck and hugged him tightly. "You were a hero today, Jonah. And you helped me. Thank you."

He looked at Summer. She smiled at him and came over and gave him a hug. "Thank you. I'll talk to you later."

CHAPTER FOURTEEN

Jonah watched Summer leave with Hunter and Polly. He wished they had a moment alone before she left. He was going to call her later. Just to make sure everything was fine when they got home. But right now, standing there on the boat dock alone, he was thankful that things had gone the way they had. They had saved a man and he just prayed that Polly was good and not traumatized. That was the strongest kid he'd ever seen.

As he walked back toward his business and apartment, he realized that his brain was not screwed on tight tonight. He turned around and went back to the boat. He went into the cabin and started to clean up. He had just been so distracted that he hadn't even thought about cleaning up or securing the boat.

He heard someone step onto the boat, felt it rock gently, and he turned toward the stairs. Summer stood there. His heart beat rapid-fire as she walked down the steps.

"I couldn't leave."

He didn't say anything; he just watched her come down the ladder and walk across the small galley and straight into his arms. He immediately wrapped his arms around her and held her gently, so very aware of what a tender and precious package she was.

He rested his chin on her hair. "Are you okay, Summer? I was so concerned for Polly and for the man that I couldn't give you the attention you needed. Are you okay?" he asked again.

She pulled back and looked up at him. "I want to know if you're okay? You were wonderful. Do you know how wonderful you were and are?"

He didn't know how to answer that.

"You knew exactly what to say to Polly. She went from crying to wanting to be a hero and to help that poor man. And, Jonah, I think she's better. Do you realize what happened today? She wanted to be closer to her mom. Fishing was what could get her there and she knew it. We took her out there and gave her what she needed. It was so beautiful and I couldn't really express to you how you touched me today, watching you give such wonderful, caring devotion to my niece. You are an amazing man. Amazing."

"I've never been called that before by a beautiful woman. I was glad to do what I could do for Polly. And if we want to talk about amazing, that is one awesome, brave, unbelievably great kid. And I'm really sorry for what happened between Hunter and Sandra. But I'm glad he's going to try to put the pain that he's been in aside and talk to her more. I think she'll do better that way. Though I think she's doing fantastic, no matter what. But to help her be healthier mentally and grow stronger and to keep the joy of her mom in her heart, I think that he will help her by sharing. Don't you? I'm not a psychologist by any means—it's just what I feel, you know?"

"I agree. But I couldn't express that to him; I couldn't get him to see what I was saying. He was just so torn up by everything. You know, the pain of learning that she was leaving him, that she no longer loved him when he loved her with all of his heart. It was so unfair what happened. And then for her to die like that, before there was any kind of resolution… Hunter's had a lot on his plate since Sandra's death. But maybe through Polly and helping her remember the good things, I don't know—maybe he can move forward. But at least Polly will get what she needs."

They stared at each other. Jonah wanted to hold her as tight as he could and never let her go. In his heart of hearts, he knew that this was the woman who would make all of his dreams come true; he just needed to be the man that she needed right now. And that meant that he had to tread very carefully.

"Jonah, would you kiss me?"

He froze and stared at her. There was so much trust and trepidation mixed in those gorgeous eyes. "Summer, are you sure you're ready to take that step?

Because I do want to kiss you. I'd be a fool to not want to kiss you but I need to know that you are sure."

"Please kiss me."

Jonah did as she asked; he lowered his head and kissed her. His heart hammered as their lips met and her arms went around his neck and he pulled her close. He was aware that he needed to be careful but he was lost to the feel of her lips kissing him back. He focused, and found his strength to pull back. He murmured, "Are you okay?"

"Yes." She gave a small, sweet laugh.

Relief washed over him, nearly making his knees weak. He had been so worried. "Good. I've never been so nervous about kissing someone. Summer, I've never wanted to kiss someone as much as I wanted to kiss you. I don't know if you know this, but I'm crazy about you."

She sniffled and he leaned back to get a better look at her. "Are you crying?"

"Yes," she whispered.

He lifted his hand and gently wiped the tears off her cheeks. "Please don't cry. I know this was hard for you. You were so shaken by what happened to you."

"I was and I think I'm still going to have problems with you approaching me from the back and I think we'll work on that. I just wasn't sure if this part would give me a problem. He didn't do anything to me other than beat me up pretty severely. But that's the only physical thing—the rest of it is all mental."

"He severely beat you?" He stared at her, stunned.

She took a deep breath. "Very badly. I didn't mention that before because it didn't seem necessary. But yes, I fought him as best I could and he didn't like that. By the time the man—my guardian angel—had appeared and helped me, I was hurt pretty bad. I had taken several major blows to the face. I had to have reconstructive surgery on my nose and my jaw was broken. So, it was not great but my eyes were okay even though they were swollen horribly. But nothing was the matter with them. To this day, my vision is perfect and I didn't have any bones around my eyes broken. I felt very blessed for that but the mental part was the lingering issue."

"Summer, I am so sorry—" Rage boiled inside

Jonah. "If I could get my hands on him I'd k—"

"No, he's not worth it." She touched his face.

"But you are," he managed, struggling to get hold of the anger like he'd never felt before pounding through him. He wanted to tear the piece of scum to pieces.

She held his gaze. "Jonah, listen to me. Meeting you and your kindness and your patience and caring with both me and Polly has been a miracle to me. I just need you to know that and I could not go home without coming here and telling you that. And kissing you. I've thought about that a lot. You were so fabulous during everything that happened today."

He hugged her tighter than before just because he couldn't hold her close enough and she seemed okay. He whispered into her hair, "I want to be the man in your life who is always your hero. I want to keep you safe."

She squeezed him tightly and nodded but didn't say anything. He worried that he might have said too much. That he was moving their relationship ahead too fast but he needed her to know that he was here to stay.

He had never been so certain of anything in all of his life. It was as if he'd known from the first moment he saw her that she was important to him.

But he couldn't come out and say that in so many words as he was afraid that might actually send her running. He would ease into telling her that he loved her.

* * *

Summer felt safe and loved in Jonah's arms. She couldn't move too fast. She couldn't tell him that she thought she was falling in love with him. She thought that by her actions and what she had said, he might hear her words and know. But she just couldn't come out and say it—couldn't rush what she was feeling. She had to make certain for both their sake that she wasn't just feeling gratitude toward him for the fact that he had helped her move past this monumental problem that she was having. It wouldn't be fair to him. And he hadn't said in so many words that he was falling for her. He was a caring, wonderful, compassionate, loving guy and this could be normal for him.

He was a protector; he might not be a fireman or policeman or EMT or a doctor or a nurse, but this man was a protector and he fixed things, like he was fixing her. But in being that caring kind of a person and being a natural hero type, of course he would want to protect her and want to help her be better. But was that love? For now, taking this slowly, step by step, was what they both needed. Because neither one of them needed to be hurt.

CHAPTER FIFTEEN

*W*hy hadn't she told him? Why had she not told him how badly she was injured? She closed her eyes and squeezed back the fear and the tears that wanted to come. She could hurt him. She knew it and she should be honest with him. She had been beaten so badly, kicked so many times in the stomach and below and then almost dead; if he had just a few more minutes, he could have easily finished her off. Her hospital stay had been long. And she had lost more than her ability to trust a man or to have people walk up from behind and touch her on the shoulder. She had lost so much more than that. She had lost the ability…

She squeezed back tears. She needed to come clean to Jonah; she needed to tell him. When she had looked into his beautiful steel-blue eyes, she hadn't been able to. She could hardly think about it herself, much less tell him, especially when she thought he was someone she wanted to have a future with.

She couldn't have a future with him if he didn't know the truth, if he didn't have a choice. As she drove away after he had walked her to her car and then gently kissed her one more time, tears flowed down her cheeks. Because she knew Jonah Sinclair, and if he knew the truth, that she couldn't have babies, he wouldn't blink an eye—he would continue seeing her anyway, not wanting to hurt her. Might even get serious but…could she trust, if their relationship got serious that in the long run he wouldn't look back and have regrets that he couldn't have children of his own? The worry hung over her.

She knew she could adopt; she would. She wanted a house full of children and just because she couldn't carry them in her womb didn't mean she couldn't love them as her own, cherish them and be the mother that they needed. Yes, she had mourned desperately that she couldn't carry her own child. She had been angry at the man for taking that from her and everything else he had taken from her, but she was trying to be grateful to be alive. She had a beautiful life ahead of her here, in this town with her brother and her darling niece. And maybe, possibly, a life with Jonah if she could trust that there would be no regrets. She had to be brave enough to tell him. And she would; she would tell him soon.

She would look into his beautiful eyes when she told him and she thought she would be able to read his initial reaction and know whether not being able to father a child of his own would be devastating to him. Or whether he could be as comfortable with adoption as she had become. Her best friend was adopted. And so very loved by her parents, who counted her the most special blessing ever in their lives.

Yes, she had to tell him the truth.

* * *

The Sunset Bay Regatta looked as if it had drawn a huge crowd. Summer and Polly wanted to arrive early so they could get seats close enough to be able to see the action. Jonah had invited them to join his mother and dad, his sisters-in-law, and Erin on the upper deck of his apartment, where they would be able to see the action very clearly.

Hunter was with them but he was on duty because Brad was on a boat and several of the other fireman were also competing on other boats. Because Hunter didn't compete and he was new, he had volunteered to work and let as many of the other guys off as they could. So he was working on a skeleton crew and he just hoped, he had told Summer, that there were no fires—at least not big fires.

She hoped that, too, because right now any of the guys working wanted to be down by the water. It was okay because the firehouse was just basically around the corner.

"Summer, Polly," someone called.

Summer glanced over to find Lila Peabody hustling toward her. Hunter stood at her back as always to prevent someone from startling her, causing her to lose it. She had almost wanted to test out the theory that she was okay but had decided that on such a public day it wouldn't be a good time to test that out.

Lila was approaching from behind, but she had hollered Summer's name and gotten her attention, so Summer was facing her now as she came to a halt in front of her. Lila's cute white hairdo was tucked behind her ears, making her eyes more vivid and sparkly. She put her hands on her hips. "I haven't seen you in the last few days. Seems like you all had a real exciting day out on the water. We heard down at Bake My Day that you and Jonah rescued someone from the water. And that you did a marvelous job. I just wanted to come and tell you how wonderful it was." She smiled at Polly. "You were there, too, and you were brave. Mr. Simpson's a friend of mine and he said that you helped take care of him. And that you were the first one to spot him in the water needing help. I think that you're just so amazing."

Summer took the hand that she held out and squeezed it tightly. "Thank you, Lila. Polly was very brave and Jonah was amazing. It wasn't something we planned but when the call came in, Jonah didn't hesitate—he knew that we needed to go. Polly was a real trooper. She got a little bitty bit scared at first but she overcame that and stepped right in to help. Is he doing okay now? We haven't heard anything in the last couple of days."

"He's doing great. They kept him overnight at the hospital but he got to come home. He just lives across the street from me, so I went over there and I took him some cake. He just bragged about y'all. The man is single—he has no one—and as you can imagine, is just eaten up with fishing. But me and the girls are all going over, just trying to take care of him."

Summer smiled. "I see. So he's single, huh?"

Lila blushed. "Yes, he is, and he's a very nice man. He would make someone a fantastic husband, I think, if he could do something about being eaten up by that fishing. You know, no woman wants a man to love fishing more than he loves her. And I have to tell you, I heard through the grapevine that that's what happened to his first wife. She left because she just couldn't take it. But you know what—I've been thinking about that and I think maybe she should have worked hard to change his mind. But that's neither here nor there."

Summer grinned. "Maybe you can change his mind because I thought on the boat he was lonely."

Polly tugged on her arm. "I asked him if he had anybody at home and he said no, he didn't. He had nobody who would be at the hospital with him. And that made me really sad. Reminded me…" She glanced up at her dad, who stared momentarily out at the water. She leaned forward and whispered, "It reminds me of my daddy. He needs to not be lonely too."

Lila clamped a hand over her mouth and Summer saw Hunter give a shake of his head. He had started to grow a little bit weary of Polly's constant worry about him being single. Summer knew that it was a sore subject and that it really bothered him, but she wasn't going to tell Polly to be quiet. Children sometimes said the things that needed to be said and Summer had just decided that what happened on that topic between Polly and her daddy was not a place she needed to be. And maybe her brother needed to listen to his daughter on that subject.

She smiled at Lila. "Maybe you could nudge him a little bit. I hear you're pretty good at nudging people in the direction you want them to go. And well, if a little birdie told him or even if he already knew or realized that fishing might have gotten in the way of his marriage, maybe the next go-around he would be willing to change things up a little bit."

Lila sighed and looked thoughtful. "You might be right. I might have to mention that to him. You know, in case one of the girls is interested in him." She shrugged and that tinge came to her cheeks again.

Summer was pretty sure that it was Lila who might be interested in her neighbor.

He was a nice man. She felt very sorry for him that day and she had thought about driving to the hospital and seeing him, but she didn't want to take Polly to the hospital. She hadn't quite gotten that far advanced and to be quite honest, Summer still had problems entering hospitals. It seemed to trigger the bad memories of what she had been through. And they didn't want to push Polly too much and she didn't want to push herself too much; it was one day at a time, little progress by little progress.

"Thanks for letting me know this. The girls are waiting for me over there in our usual spot. I think I see some gals up on top of Jonah's deck, looking interested in y'all. Surely, he invited you to come up there. His deck won't hold everybody but it will hold his family and the important people in his life."

Summer let that sink in and hoped her cheeks didn't turn pink. But from the heat that she felt in them, she was pretty sure that she now looked like Lila had looked moments before. "Well, actually, yes, we are supposed to go up there."

"He invited us because he said he would like us to see him and from up there we would be able to see almost the whole race." Polly jumped up and down and clapped her hands and giggled. "I'm very excited."

Moments later, they walked up the stairs. Erin, Lulu and Rosie greeted them. She'd thought they would meet Cassie, Jonah's sister who was the photographer but she hadn't been able to make it after all.

"You're going to have to come by my place and play with the dogs and puppies we watch all day," Lulu told Polly.

"You have dogs?"

Lulu grinned. "I watch them at my doggy daycare. They always enjoy someone to play with."

"Can we go see them?" Polly asked Hunter.

"Sure, if you and Summer don't get to go by one day I'll take you."

"I can take her, that sounds fun." Summer loved dogs and hoped they would get one soon.

"Perfect." Lulu smiled. "They're going to love you."

"Come over here by the railing," Erin said, and led them across the large deck. "You'll be able to see the race from here."

"I can't wait," Polly said, holding onto the top beam and looking through the slats that were too close together to have to worry about her falling through.

Rosie pointed. "We have a seat set up over there for you, Polly. There's binoculars for you to watch even more of the adventure that's going to happen out there."

"See them right down there," Erin pointed at the boat holding all the brothers. "They're all lined up and getting ready. Aren't the boats all beautiful?"

Polly beamed. "Jonah told me that the boats all run off manpower and sail power. No motor power."

"That's about right," Polly agreed. "They all have to work together and they're really good at it. But there's some stiff competition. It's been a long time since they did this together as a team."

Summer had moved immediately toward the corner of the deck, just subtly moving her back so she knew where everyone was.

Hunter came to stand beside her. "Rosie, I don't know if I've had a chance to tell you that I love your baked goods. Brad's been picking up all those muffins in the morning and bringing them to the firehouse and I'm addicted. He brings an assortment but I favor the marmalade ones. You know, the ones with the cinnamon and stuff on them. Boy, those are delicious."

"That's one of my all-time favorites. Kind of built my career on them and a few others. I'm glad you like them. We're glad you're here and glad you brought this beautiful lady with you, and this darling little girl."

"We're happy to be here. And your family is great. We're very grateful to Jonah for everything he's done for Polly."

Rosie smiled and her gaze touched Summer. "We are very fond of Jonah. He's special. And we are excited that you two seem to have hit it off." She winked at Summer.

Polly grinned. "We are too. I hope that my Aunt Summer and Jonah get married."

Everybody gave a startled laugh, especially Summer. Polly was getting braver and braver with everything she said. "Polly speaks her mind. Polly, we have to move slowly. I like Jonah very much and Jonah likes me very much, but we haven't known each other all that long. So don't go jumping the gun."

Polly grinned. "I'm not. I'm going to go over there and look through my binoculars. And see how they look up close."

Hunter looked at Rosie. "I don't know if you've noticed this but my daughter...I sometimes wonder if she's an old person in a little bitty body."

Rosie grinned. "It's okay; she's good. Believe me, I understand that these things go slow. I was just letting you know that everybody here was thrilled. As you move around and meet the rest of our family—my mother-law and dad-in-law—don't be surprised if you don't get more conversations like this. I'm just trying to ease the blow for you."

Erin added, "They all have high expectations because Jonah hasn't had interest in dating for a very long time and we're just excited." She nodded her head toward the older woman in conversation at the far end of the deck. "That beautiful lady down there is our mom. And she desperately wants her kids married and a house full of babies. So don't let her run you off. The three of us as of now—well, you know I'm getting married but Adam and Brad have married these wonderful ladies, Rosie and Lulu. I have a wonderful man who happens to be in New York at the moment, meeting with his publishers. But I can't wait for you to meet him. He's—according to me and as far as I'm concerned—the most amazing man in the world." She laughed. "I don't know if you can tell but I'm crazy in love with the man. But, anyway, don't feel pressure from my mom. She won't be able to contain herself. Believe me, none of us have announced that we are having babies but she's already buying baby clothes. And she's already talking about what room in the house she's going to change into the nursery for when we have our babies and they come to stay with Grandma."

"Those are just subtle hints from her that it's baby time," Rosie added, her eyes twinkling happily as she and Erin looked at each other.

Summer thought they looked almost as if they had a secret.

"She's like a bulldozer," Erin chuckled. "But she means well."

Summer's stomach had dropped to her toes. She met Hunter's gaze and he dipped his chin; she could see in his eyes he was telling her to hold on and not overreact. She saw sympathy there; he knew what she was thinking about. In the traditional sense of the word, she wouldn't be able to give Jonah's mother what she had her heart set on. She had to keep reminding herself that she could do it in other ways. All she needed was approval and she could adopt.

Her head had started to hurt. And her mouth was dry. She fought off the sensation of inadequacy and the deep issues that she had had to fight so hard to let go of. Told herself all the positives: she could adopt; she didn't have any expectations anymore and she could make it through anyone else's expectations. Everyone was jumping to conclusions—because Jonah might not be falling for her like she was thinking. *What if he didn't mind but what if his parents did?*

What was she thinking? She knew no person in their right mind would care whether a child was adopted or whether a child came from two people who loved each other's flesh and bone. But it was just the mind game that she didn't have the option. *This was ridiculous.*

"I'll try not to let her intimidate me."

Hunter had reached out and taken her elbow. "Do you need to sit down?"

"You look pale," Lulu said.

"Lulu is right," Rosie said, alarmed.

Erin instantly strode across the deck and returned within seconds with a glass of iced tea. "Here, drink this." She placed the glass in Summer's hand and Summer took a sip.

"I'm fine. I don't know what came over me. I just had a weak spell."

Rosie grabbed a chair from a table behind her. "Here, sit right here. We would never hear the end of it if we let something happen to you while Jonah was out there." She looked at Hunter. "Does she do this often? I mean, I don't mean to talk over you but you are flushed really bad and now you are so pale—there is no color in your skin."

Hunter knelt in front of her and took her hands. "Take deep breaths. Come on, breathe. Just concentrate on breathing. She has panic attacks sometimes and I think she was on the verge of one. Come on…count for me—count backward."

Summer focused on her brother. "Ten, nine, eight…" She counted slowly, concentrating on her brother, nothing else: strictly on her brother and the counting. She felt her pulse slow and her erratic heartbeat started to calm down. And she could breathe again. "One." She made it to the last number and smiled at him. "Thank you. I feel more in control now. I'm so sorry I worried y'all." She hadn't told them her story; she hadn't done what Jonah had told her to do— to let people in town know her history so they could support her and understand what she was going through. But could she tell them now?

Yes, a small voice in her mind yelled very loudly. "I will have to tell you later—not tonight—why I have panic attacks."

Rosie placed her hand on her shoulder and Erin smiled compassionately. Rosie squeezed her shoulder. "We will be there for you when you feel like you can tell us whatever it is that's bothering you. Because obviously if something we said triggered a panic attack, then we need to understand it so that maybe we cannot do that again. Or, as your friends, maybe we can help you through it. And know what to do for you."

Erin agreed, nodding. "She's exactly right. Hunter, aren't you getting off your schedule tomorrow? I mean, aren't you on the same schedule that Brad's on?"

"Yes, I am."

"Then that means you'll have some time to take care of Polly?"

"Yes, I will."

"Good. Then what if we have coffee tomorrow? Why don't you and Rosie come to the B&B tomorrow? If we go to the coffee shop like most people go to have a talk, Rosie will never have any peace. There will be so many people there who want a piece of her, we will never get to talk to her. So we can come and sit around my kitchen island, have coffee and some of her muffins that she'll bring with her, and you can tell us. Girl talk—you're new in town and you haven't had any girl time. How does that sound?"

Summer blinked back tears. She had been so emotional lately. "It sounds wonderful."

"Good." Rosie winked at her. "It's always good to have friends and we want to be that for you, so I'm looking forward to that. Now, do you want to watch this race? Are you up to it? We can move that chair over to the railing so you can see."

"I can't be there tomorrow," Lulu said. "But maybe next time. Don't forget though, come by any time."

Feeling a little bit better, Summer nodded and then went to stand. "I think I'm great. I will go stand by the railing and watch."

Hunter stood, too, and together they all walked to the edge just as the gun fired and the race began.

CHAPTER SIXTEEN

Summer watched as the boats moved out of the bay. She wasn't sure how they worked; she had never really looked into sailing but they moved out into the bay and then obviously had a course on their electronic device so they knew where they were sailing. As the sails went up, she watched Jonah on his boat and his brothers as they moved to get the sails up. The large sail fluttered in the wind, caught the wind, and then the boat moved forward.

Maryetta and Leo came down to where Summer and Hunter were watching the race. Hunter gently touched her elbow so that she would know someone was approaching, so she turned as they reached her. Maryetta was beaming, smiling profusely as she approached Summer. Summer tried to prepare herself for more conversations similar to what she had already been through. If what Rosie and Erin had said was true and they suspected that she and Jonah were interested in each other, she very well might get the same conversations again and she did not need to have another panic attack. She smiled at the older couple.

"Hi, I'm Summer. Thank you for inviting me to spend this time up here with your family."

"And I'm Hunter and that's my daughter, Polly. We're very glad to be here."

Jonah's mother tsked away their thank-yous. "We're just glad you are here. We'd fit everybody up here if there was room. But we were thrilled that Jonah invited you to join us. My son seems to be very fond of you and your niece. And Brad says you're doing an excellent job at the firehouse, Hunter. He needed more help desperately. So we're very thankful you're here and that you brought Summer and Polly with you."

"By the way, just for introductions, I'm Leo and this is my wife, Maryetta, Jonah's mom. I figured you already knew that but I'm just making sure."

Erin leaned over from where she stood and smiled. "It's not as though you couldn't tell by the resemblance who they were. We all look in some way or another like we belong to the both of them."

What Erin said was exactly true. All of the kids she had met so far had some resemblance to one or both of them. "Well, I'm glad we came here, too. This beautiful town is not Houston—when I first moved out to Houston, I enjoyed the more cosmopolitan feel of it, in a more Texas laid-back way, but I'm over that now and I'm loving this small town. I'm so glad I made the decision to come."

Maryetta raised a brow. "It didn't take Jonah very long to decide that he was glad you were here. I know, I know...you already heard, I'm sure, my kids are going crazy over the fact that I'm eager to have grandchildren and for my thirty-yearish-old children to get married. At the first of the year, none of my children were married and it was just ridiculous. You'd think a mother of six kids would have somebody get married in their early twenties so that I would have had grandkids for ten years now. But no, no, no—not mine.

"So, anyway, I got a little bit anxious, so I started telling them that I was really anxious and somehow or another...you know how they always say that if you have a goal and you speak it into the world, it's better for it to come true? Well, that's exactly what happened. I said it to my kids and then, boom! It was just almost instantly that Rosie showed up to sweep my son Adam off his feet. It's just been wonderful and then Lulu—that darling Lulu with her puppy heaven and all that stuff—she was already here but did my Brad even notice? No. But not long after I made my wishes known, the two of them got together. Of course, it took a fire but we're not going to talk about that part of it."

"Fire?"

"Yes. It took fire to get his attention. But he wasn't the only one lollygagging around. Erin was doing it too but now she has her handsome author fiancé...I'm hoping that the husband part comes quickly because the quicker the marriage, the quicker the babies. One of these three is going to give me a baby before the end of the year. I think they're just trying to hold out for spite."

"Surely not," Summer didn't know what to say and probably shouldn't have said that. But she was feeling a bit desperate.

She chuckled. "I hope no. But anyway, I'm thrilled that Jonah is finally showing signs of coming out of this self-proclaimed time of aloneness. He used to date and then he just stopped. I was floored because I just knew he was going to be my first child to marry." She looked out at the water.

Summer wanted very badly to glance over her shoulder and see what was going on in the boat race but she didn't want to be rude, either. She would love it if they started talking about the boat race and not all these personal things about Jonah and his love life or the fact that Maryetta really wanted grandchildren.

"I can understand your frustrations. And I have also heard that saying that if you speak it, it's going to happen quicker. So I'm glad it's working for you. But

Jonah and I—we're basically friends who are getting to know each other." There, maybe that would help ease some of this tension that she was feeling coming from Maryetta. My goodness, she had three kids married now or nearly married, so surely Jonah didn't need to be feeling any pressure.

And to be honest, she didn't want Jonah to feel pressure to get married. She wanted Jonah to want to get married because he wanted to get married, not because his mother wanted him to get married and have kids. And then there was that issue with the children. She tried not to think about that.

Thankfully, Maryetta squealed with delight and clapped her hands. It gave Summer the excuse to spin toward the water just in time to see, out in the distance on the horizon, Jonah's boat pull into the lead. They rode parallel to the bay, racing toward a yellow float on the horizon. At least that's what it looked like to her; she really had no clue. But she was excited to see that they were now in the lead.

From where Polly was, Polly pulled the binoculars from her eyes and yelled excitedly, "I can see Jonah on board and he's working so hard and his brothers are, too! I wish I was on that boat."

Hunter gave a dry laugh. "Not on that boat for a good long while yet. We're just getting used to you being on the water."

Polly frowned. "I know, Daddy, but you know I'm going to be a boat woman and a fisherwoman like my mama when I grow up. So I'm going to have to get used to all these boats. That boat goes really fast and I love the sail. Look how it's pushing out up there at the top—that's the wind, right?"

Leo was the one who answered. "Yes, dear, that is. And the wind's blowing good out there. It's catching the sail. My boys know how to utilize the wind to its best. One day, when you are able to go out on that boat, you'll really enjoy it but right now, from what I understand, you're doing good getting on a boat like you did with Jonah this week."

"I am. And it was fun. And I caught a lot of fish. And I got to see Aunt Summer and Jonah smiling at each other a lot. And then we saved that man. It's been great."

Leo chuckled. "You did?"

"You are adorable," Maryetta said and then looked at Hunter and asked softly, "Are you sure that person in that little bitty body is only five?"

"Yes, ma'am, last I checked, that's still my daughter and yes, she's going on about thirty, I think, if not older."

Summer knew that part of her maturing was what she had been through; that would grow a child up very quickly. She smiled at Polly. "You are a jewel, darling. Now yank those binoculars back up to your eyes and tell me what Jonah's doing. They're still in the lead, aren't they?"

Polly did what she was asked; she put the binoculars to her eyes and then studied the horizon for a little bit. And then she looked at her. "Yes, he's doing good. He's at the wheel and he looks very serious."

Summer smiled inwardly. She knew that Jonah would be serious about this race. She had talked to him briefly on the boat ride and he was hoping that he and his brothers could win this like the old days. He wanted this for them as a bond. And she hoped for his sake that it happened, too. And she had to say that the man was so amazing and obviously his brothers were, too, because as the boat cut around the second yellow float and pulled ahead, it looked as if it were growing the distance between it and the other boats. She smiled to herself. She hadn't expected anything less. She got the feeling that when Jonah Sinclair set his mind on something, he got what he wanted. Whether it was by challenging hard work or just plain stubborn persistence. And she liked that about him.

* * *

They had all gone down from the deck and to the dock, where everyone had gathered around near the podium as The Sunset Bay Regatta Sailing Cup had been awarded to the Sinclair brothers for the first time in several years. Everyone cheered for them and Summer thought it was the sweetest thing. They laughed and joked and teased the audience as they took the award and held it up high. All the other competitors laughed and it was easy to see that there was no major vendettas or grudge competition happening here. It was all in good fun and she loved that. She loved that this town seemed to be better than anything she could have imagined.

She laughed as she looked over her shoulder at Hunter. "This place is amazing. I'm so glad you came here."

Her brother grinned at her. "I am, too. Now are you going to go up there and get a kiss from your new man?"

She frowned at him. "Oh, Hunter, not you too."

He laughed. "I couldn't help it. After all the pressure his family was putting on you up on that deck, I just couldn't believe it. But I have to admit, you're standing there with a large grin on your face as you watch him. I've never seen you look at anybody like you look at him. And I'm just telling you right now that I hope you don't let what happened to you stop you from reaching for happiness. I know you've got a lot going on, but he's a good guy and I can't imagine anything you have wrong with you that he's not going to be okay with and work with you on. If the look I see on your face and the look I see on his face when he looks at you equals what I think it does."

They were trying to talk rather quietly because Polly was chattering to a little girl standing next to her and her family; they'd had a little bit of distraction for her as they spoke.

Now she leaned back where she could talk to him more quietly. "I don't know. I think about it all the time. And you heard some of the conversation they had earlier about having children. Goodness, talk about pressure. How will his parents react when they find out that he's pursuing someone who can't give him a child?"

Her brother's face hardened. "Anybody who would look at you with anything other than compassion is nothing in my book. I have no sympathy for them, and I can't imagine that nice lady and man we met earlier would ever think anything bad. You cannot help what happened to you or what it stole from you. It's not your fault that you were hurt so terribly bad. You have to learn to deal with that and accept it."

She stared at him. "I have accepted it."

"Have you? Because, Summer, I love you but," he leaned closer, practically whispering, "I think if you really had accepted it, you wouldn't even be questioning what Jonah or his parents think about you not being able to bear a child."

Summer couldn't believe what her brother was saying. She stepped away from him. "I can't believe you're saying that to me. I have accepted it."

Her brother stiffened, his eyes looking over her shoulder.

"Accepted what?" Jonah asked from behind her.

She spun around. "Jonah. I didn't hear you come up."

"Jonah!" Polly spun around from talking with the little girl to find Jonah standing there. She threw herself into his arms. "You did so good. I watched through the binoculars and I could see everything you were doing and it was so cool."

"Hey, kiddo, thanks. My brothers and I worked as a team and we got it done. It's unbelievable that we were able to after not practicing for so many years but

I guess we still have it." He grinned at Hunter and Summer. "We had a little bit of a rough patch getting started but as soon as the wind caught that sail finally like it needed to, we took off. It was great. Thank you so much for coming." His smile dimmed. "Summer, tell me—is something wrong?"

"No, nothing. It was great. We loved being here."

He studied her. "Did you ride into town with this cute little girl in my arms and your brother?"

"Yes, she did," Hunter said.

"Well, if you don't mind, I'd like to give Summer a ride home tonight."

"That would be great," Hunter said.

Summer looked at her brother. "Hunter, I can talk for myself."

He laughed. "Yeah, I know you can. But I think that tonight I couldn't help myself—I just wanted to give you a little push, if you know what I mean."

She fought to not glare at him because she knew exactly what he meant. He wanted her to have time alone with Jonah so she could tell him everything that had happened to her when she had been harassed and attacked.

"I will be glad for you to take me home, Jonah."

"Great. But first, let's celebrate. Everybody's got their stores open and we've got the usual crowd here for the annual festivals. If you want a cheesecake on a stick or some caramel crazy corn or some buttery pretzels or anything like that, it's right here. If you want a muffin, you'll have to go to the muffin shop because tonight was the night that Rosie took off to watch Adam compete. Y'all come over here to get some, where the family is."

And with that, Jonah set Polly on the ground and placed his hand in Summer's, and they walked toward where Brad, Tate, Adam, and the entire family were gathered around, chatting and laughing with all the locals. Lila was there, and Birdie and Doreen and Mami, and a whole bunch of other people. She wasn't sure she could recall their names if she was given a test, but one day she would learn everyone's name.

"Hey, so I guess you all saw the race." Brad laughed as he hugged Lulu close and grinned over her red hair. "The Sinclairs are back. All we have to do is convince Tate here to move back for good and, man, we could enter all kinds of competitions."

Hunter slapped him on the back. "Well, Chief, I think you did good but I wouldn't push my luck if I were you. It depends on your competition, if you know what I mean?"

Brad grinned at Hunter, and Summer was glad to see the way the two got along. "Are you telling me that if the competition had been stiffer, that me and my brothers wouldn't have won?"

Hunter grinned. "See there—you are a smart guy. That's exactly what I was saying."

"Well then, if that's the case, then maybe you need to start practicing up and get you a team to see if you could up the competition level next year. Seeing as how you're now a Sunset Bay transplanted citizen."

"Well, don't mind if I do. First, I'm going to have to learn to sail. So I'm going to need you to give me some lessons. How does that sound?"

"I think I can fit it in to my busy schedule."

Summer laughed and Jonah squeezed her arm gently and whispered in her ear, "I think your brother has my brother's number. I think they know exactly how to push each other's buttons. That's good they get along."

"Yes, it is, and I am so glad because my brother needs that. He needs it so bad. I can't wait for him to have healed enough to maybe find someone new to maybe not fall in love with but at least date. He spends too much time in the house. Thankfully, when he's at the firehouse with all of the guys, he has people to be around and not just me and Polly."

"Well, Brad says he's a great hand and I'm sure everything will work out in its own time. Kind of like between you and me."

She stared at him, her heart pounding. Her brother was right; she had to tell him. Tonight.

* * *

As Jonah walked Summer toward his truck later that evening, he placed his arm over her shoulders and tugged her close to his side. She had looked a little tense toward the end of the evening and he was really wanting to talk to her. "So now that we're alone, what's bothering you?"

"Bothering me? Nothing."

He looked down at her. "Well, Summer, I hate to tell you this, but I don't believe you. Something's bothering you. Are you rethinking our kiss?"

She stopped walking and turned to him. She placed her hand on his heart, looking up at him.

He still had his arm around her and he searched her eyes for any sign that what she was saying was not the truth. But he couldn't see anything; he just saw the questioning look there. "If that's not what it is, what's wrong?"

"I don't want to take what happened between us for granted. I mean, we kissed. And we admitted that we have feelings for each other but I don't want to jump the gun and say something out of order. But I really have to tell you that I wasn't completely truthful about how badly I was injured when I was attacked."

His gut tightened and anger rolled through him at this person who had attacked Summer. "You were hurt worse, weren't you?" The words were almost a growl.

He hated to hear what she had to say.

She nodded. And paled. "I was."

He looked around. People were still milling around. "Okay, this really isn't a good place to have this conversation. Come on. Let's get in the truck and I'll drive us somewhere we can talk."

They got in the truck; he pulled away from the curb and drove out of town. Tension filled the space between them. His mind rolled, trying to figure out how bad it was; it was a nightmare to think that she could have been terribly injured. And why hadn't she told him before?

He reached a dirt path and pulled off on it. The truck emerged on a secluded beach. He parked facing the water and then he turned toward her. "Do you want to get out and walk on the beach?"

"Yes, I do."

"Okay. I think that's good." He got out and hurried around to open her door but she was already out, waiting for him. He took her hand and, hand in hand, they walked past the scraggly grass and onto the white sugar sand. His thoughts were still whirling as he went through all kinds of scenarios. "Okay, you can tell me anything. You know that, right?"

He feared that she had been actually raped and she just hadn't told him. And the fact that she hadn't told him made him sick to think she had been afraid to tell him. Why wouldn't she tell him something like that?

She didn't say anything at first, just kept walking, and he walked beside her. The waves were rolling in and easing out. It was a gentle and mesmerizing rushing of water and there was a nice breeze. He just tried to concentrate on that and not the turmoil going on inside him as he gave her time to tell him what she needed to say.

"I was injured really bad. The man—my guardian angel—he didn't get there until I had been beaten severely. I fought but I ended up with terrible injuries. In the end, he didn't rape me—my guardian angel got there in time. But…" She paused and turned to look at him. "I need to tell you this because it matters. You need to know this before you get in any deeper with me, before you possibly end up falling in love with me. You need to know that because of my injuries, I can't have children of my own. I'll never be able to carry a child of yours…if you were to fall in love with me and we were to become a couple."

He just stared at her. The impact of what she said settled through him, making his stomach sick at what she must have suffered, how horribly she must have been kicked. It just made him want to cry. He had no words at first. He wrapped his arms around her, pulled her to his chest, cupped her head with his hand and gently stroked her thick, soft hair. "It's going to be okay, Summer. It's going to be okay. You can adopt."

She went still against him. "I can. But I just need you to know what you would be giving up. If you got involved with me."

He closed his eyes and fought the anger at the man who had done this to her and fought to find the compassion he felt for Summer and the love he had for her and to let that win out so she could only feel that emotion in him. She didn't need to feel the anger that he harbored for this piece of junk who had hurt her so.

"Summer, darling, there's only one flaw with your sweet notion to try to help me. I'm already in love with you. I fell hard and fast probably the very first time I saw you and we were eating ice cream together on the dock with our little matchmaker Polly. It's been rough not being able to tell you that but there was no way I could rush that and scare you off. And if I'm scaring you off right now, then I'll take it all back and pretend it never happened and we'll go slow and steady and all that good stuff. But if you're trying to protect me from falling in love with you and wanting to marry you, you're too late. It's already a done deal, darling. I want to marry you. I want to adopt a house full of babies with you. I want it all. With you. Only you."

She couldn't believe what she was hearing. Tears streamed down her face. "I'm overwhelmed. I love you too. I just have to be fair to you. I can't take advantage of you—I can't."

"You're not taking advantage of me. This is what I want. And if I have to wait for you for however long, I will wait because I've never felt like this for anyone and I'll never feel like this for anyone. And a child with you is a child with you. I love you. I'm grateful I found you. I'm with you. I'll stand by you, from here to eternity."

Tears streamed down her face as he bent his head and kissed her.

Summer couldn't believe what was happening. She was in the moment right now but she was going to have to think hard about this. Could she really let him do this? Could she?

CHAPTER SEVENTEEN

As she kissed Jonah back and he let his love flow through her, filling her with a cleansing power that she had been so afraid she would never feel, she tried to believe him when he said that not having his own child wouldn't matter to him. *Had her brother been telling the truth? Was it her who hadn't accepted what happened to her?*

She broke the kiss. And smiled at Jonah tenderly with emotion that she wasn't quite sure how to express or what she was exactly feeling. Turmoil rolled inside her, making her stomach feel ill and her knees weak.

"Jonah, I love you too. And because I love you, I just don't know if this is right. I have a lot on my plate. I have a lot of things going on in my head. And the more I think about it, it might not be fair to you at all."

He stared at her as if not being able to comprehend what she was saying. "Summer, you're just overthinking this. You've been through a terrible situation. And yes, you have issues that I'm sure you still have to overcome. It's not going to come easy and you can already tell that I'll help you. We'll work together."

"I know you will. But I don't want to go too fast. And I really do want you to think about this. I'm not going to hold you to what you said. Okay? So you need to be sure. And I'm going to do what you said, though; I'm going to have coffee with your sister and Rosie tomorrow. And I'm going to be truthful with them. I'm going to tell them everything, like you said that I should. This is a wonderful town and I think I'm in a good place. So you don't have to be worried about me, and you don't have to tell me things…that you might not truly mean."

"Summer, I meant every word that I said. I don't say things I don't mean. That's not me."

"But Jonah, I know you. You're the best man I've ever met. You would do anything to help anyone and I just need to make sure that what you're saying to me is the truth and not just because you are compassionate and want to help me. Please think about this. Your mother tonight—they really want grandchildren—"

"My mother doesn't matter in this. I'm compassionate for my mother and her want for a grandchild, but what's happening right now is between you and me. My mother does not enter into this conversation. I love you and I want to adopt as many kids as you want to. And if I don't have a biological child of my own, that's okay."

She stared at him, wanting so much to believe him. But also knowing that he needed time. He didn't need to commit to something like this right off the bat. "We're going to still go slow and you're going to have time to think about this."

He looked as if he couldn't believe what she was saying. "We're going to go slow for your sake but I'm not taking anything back. I've spoken the truth."

She cupped his cheek. "And I love you for that. But I cannot take a chance on you regretting this one day. I need time."

"I can understand that. I just don't understand why you don't think I know what I want."

"I can't explain it. But I think right now I need to go home. It's been a long day. I'm so glad you won your race. But I think I'm ready to go to sleep. My brain's tired."

It was a lame excuse to leave but she needed some reason to let this conversation end tonight so they could have some distance from it. Last thing she was going to do tonight was sleep, but at least he nodded and then took her hand and they walked back to the truck. She was still thinking about how startled he looked, long after he left her at the door of Hunter's home.

* * *

The next day, Jonah got up early and went for a jog.

He was still in shock about Summer's response to him. He was jogging down the south end of the beach when his brother Tate fell into step beside him.

"Morning, Jonah. Thought I'd find you out here. Just out here getting my exercise while I'm in town—you know, staying in shape. What are you doing? You don't normally jog, do you?" Tate was always the jokester. Always kidding Jonah about his amazing physique and Jonah's regular guy physique.

Jonah laughed despite the emotions running through him. "Hey, brother, you don't get these muscles that I have by just taking care of boats and fishing. I have to jog every once in a while to keep the pizza off my hips." He grinned at him.

Tate grinned back. "Well, I'm glad to see you're doing that because I was starting to think you're gonna get yourself a little inner-tube around that hip, you know what I mean? And with that gorgeous woman you had on your arm last night, I was gonna give you some tips on how to keep her."

Jonah frowned. He knew his brother was joking but right now his brain was so stormy.

"What's wrong, Jonah? I was just joking, you know. But she is gorgeous. We're all happy to see you maybe have somebody special. Why, that look of—I don't know what that look is that you've got on your face. Are you mad?"

He concentrated on his feet, the steps pounding by as they ran on the hard-packed wet sand. The waves crashed in the early morning; seagulls were flying overhead and the sun was just starting to rise above the sea line. "I don't know, Tate. I told Summer how I feel about her last night and I can't go into it, but she has a background that she's dealing with that she's having to get some help with. She was hurt once, really bad—like physically hurt. But she hasn't told anybody in town that other than me, so it's not like I can just go talk to anybody about it. But since you are leaving soon, I don't see why I can't at least use you as a sounding board.

"I think she might be going to actually tell Rosie and Erin today. They're having coffee with her, thank goodness. She needs friends in town. She moved here and she knows no one—all she knows is Hunter and

Polly. And me. I met her getting ice cream on the dock and I've been crazy about her ever since I first laid eyes on her. But Tate, I'm in love with her. I'm sinking like a rock here and when I told her that last night—" He stopped running and raked a hand through his hair and stared at Tate, who had stopped jogging a couple of steps ahead of him.

Tate turned to look at him. He put his hands on his hips. "What's wrong? What did she say?"

"She said I'm too nice of a guy and that she thinks that I'm only telling her I love her because I am a nice guy. She's afraid I'm not feeling what I'm actually saying I'm feeling. Something like that. I haven't slept hardly at all. She's all I can think of. But y'all tease me about being a nice guy. What's wrong with being a nice guy? I mean, I try to do right. I try to treat people nice. I try to do anything I can for anybody and everybody, you know, just being a good neighbor. And then I fall for somebody and I'm nice to her and now she thinks I don't know my mind. She's using my niceness against me—it is just wrong."

"She's trying to protect you."

Jonah turned to stare out at the ocean, watching the crashing waves and feeling like his whole world was crashing down with them. "Yeah, she is. But I want to protect her. She was attacked—she was hurt. I want to be there for her, to protect her with my life if I have to. How do I get her to understand that?"

"She must have had something really serious happen to her to make her so wary. But what is she trying to protect you from?"

"She was attacked and beaten so badly and kicked so horrendously she can't have children. And she thinks that matters to me. She thinks that I might regret one day not being able to father my own child. But Tate, I can adopt—we can adopt. She's fine with that for herself; she's grateful that she has the option. And she will be a wonderful mother. She'll adopt all these children or as many as she can—I don't know how many she will adopt. She may only adopt one, who knows? But I have a feeling that she's going to have a house full of kids. And you know me—I would have a house full. But she's afraid that I'm just telling her that I love her to be nice. And that in the end I may regret this and she is, like you say, protecting me."

Tate stared out at the ocean and shook his head, thinking. He turned to look at Jonah.

Jonah had been watching him and he grimaced. "I want to go there and demand that she just listen to me. But I need to be patient."

"Yeah, you're right. Maybe you do need to be patient. You know, y'all haven't known each other very long. Maybe when she realizes the truth after she's adjusted to her life herself then maybe you two can have a future together."

He raked a hand through his hair, closed his eyes, and breathed in the salty damp air. And told himself he needed to do just that—take his time. Not get all bent out of shape just because she hadn't reacted to his first proposal in the right manner. In time, she would come to know that he meant what he said. He opened his eyes and nodded at his brother. "Okay, you're right. I'm going to be patient. I'm going to pull back and I'm going to wait. Thanks."

"I'll send you a bill later. Now, let's get back to this run. Because I have a feeling that you really needed it this morning. Come on, let's go."

Jonah took off after Tate, knowing that he was right. He had come to the decision that he would wait. He would be patient; he wouldn't push. But that didn't ease the tension in him. Hopefully jogging miles or as long as his brother Mr. Superhero pushed him would ease up some of the tension; it would exhaust him and then maybe he could get through the day. He'd be too tired to think. And he'd be patient. That was going to be hard. But for Summer, he was going to do it.

* * *

Erin's bed-and-breakfast was beautiful. From the moment Summer stepped through the front door into the older home that had been decorated to perfection, she felt at home. The place looked as though it had come straight out of a magazine and it was gorgeous. "You must be an interior designer. This is amazing."

Erin smiled. "I studied pictures. You wouldn't believe how many magazines I searched through and online to finally come up with just what I wanted. And

I'm very pleased with it, so thank you. I'm very proud of my place and I'm just so happy when people react the way you do to it. That's what I wanted—I wanted people to come in and feel special, feel like they were staying somewhere that they could be pampered but be at home too."

"You have succeeded."

Rosie stuck her head out of the kitchen door. "I think it's amazing too. I told her when I get my house built, she's going to have to come help me. I mean, I'm semi talented but this is gorgeous. So, come on back. We're going to have coffee and I brought muffins."

Erin let Summer go ahead of her and they entered the kitchen, which was like a chef's kitchen, even though it wasn't gigantic. The French-country white cabinets, stainless-steel gas stove and two ovens, and blue-and-white checked barstools around the gorgeous granite countertop were so pretty. They all sat down. Rosie poured their coffee and waved Erin out of the way, telling her to sit down and enjoy.

Erin laughed and took a seat at the counter with Summer. "My sister-in-law is pushy. She just takes over, like it's her coffee shop."

Rosie winked at Summer. "I like to pamper people and Erin pampers people all the time, so I'm just here to do that for her. I can be bossy when it comes to that."

Erin tilted her head toward her sister-in-law. "You pamper people all day long, too—not just me. You do it more than I do. You have I don't know how many people come through your Bake My Day bakery and I have—well, it's growing but I have slow spots, you know, so I need to be pampering you."

Summer watched the two and felt her heart swell. She really liked them. And she was so grateful they had invited her over. She just needed someone to talk to. She had had a hard time sleeping. She had finally slept, mostly from exhaustion, but she hadn't had peaceful dreams; she had tossed and turned.

"Now—we're here to talk to you." Rosie took a seat and pushed the plate of amazing-looking muffins in front of her.

She picked out a strawberry muffin and, needing something to do with her hands, she broke it in two and laid it on the plate in front of her. "When I came here, I had been hurt. That's why I came with my brother and Polly—because I needed to get away from Houston and the memories of what had happened to me there. But I didn't feel comfortable telling anybody about my past. Then I met Jonah and I just opened up to him, and I told him what had happened to me. He urged me to let other people know so that other people could help me but I told him I couldn't do it. I think that's been a little bit unfair to him because you know how nice Jonah is. He's just the most wonderful person—wonderful man. I think, because no one else knew other than my brother, that he felt a sense of responsibility toward me. And he told me that I should tell everyone and y'all would have my back, too, just like he does and y'all would help me."

Erin laid her hand on her arm. "Of course, we will. He's completely right. And you're completely right, too—he's an amazing, wonderful person. But what happened to you?"

Rosie gave her an empathetic smile. "You know we'll do whatever we can to help you."

She closed her eyes and nodded as she prepared to tell them. And try not to have a panic attack while she did. "I was attacked in the parking garage. A man attacked me from behind. I fought and he beat me up terribly. It hurt me very badly, physically—broke bones and messed my face up.

"But I have nightmares and I have psychological fears, too. I can't be approached from behind. Your brother's been good about doing what Hunter does. Hunter trails me, basically, to prevent anyone from sneaking up on me—you know, just coming up behind me and touching my shoulder will just totally throw me into hysterics. It's ridiculous and crazy—not crazy…that's a terrible word. It's just hard for me. I'm not a weak person, so it's been really hard for me to accept that I have this leftover problem. Now, when I'm with Jonah, he does the same thing. So, Hunter and Jonah protect me but they told me that I should tell someone else and get it off my chest and that people won't look down on me, but they would also look out for me. That people would get used to not approaching me from the back until I get over this. I see someone—

a doctor—he helps me. I'm getting there, I think, but it's more than that. I needed to tell y'all, so that it's a trust thing. But I also can't have children. I just recently told Jonah that horrendous part of the story."

Rosie and Erin both looked terribly upset.

Rosie was the first to speak, tears glistening in her eyes. "I am so sorry that happened to you and to not be able to have children because of that. Did he rape you?"

"No, he didn't. I fought and he just hurt me. Another man came and got there in time to save me—rescue me—and ran the guy off. Well, he hurt the guy and the guy got arrested. His trial is in a few very short weeks and I'm going to go and speak. Confront him."

"Are you going to be able to do that?" Erin asked.

"I am. Hunter's going to go with me. I feel like it's what I need to do. I need to speak for all those who have been wronged like I was and didn't get the chance to confront their assailants. And I think that it might help me to move forward. My doctors do, too."

"I think that's very brave of you. And can we come to give you some support, too?" Rosie asked.

235

Erin nodded. "We would more than love to do that. Because Jonah was right—you've got friends now and we want to support you."

"I hadn't even thought of that. But it might be terrible. I hate to ask you to do that."

"You didn't ask—we're offering. I bet Jonah will be there."

She wasn't so sure about that. She wasn't even sure Jonah would speak to her after the way she treated him last night. "I don't know if he will be. I told him that we were moving too fast and that he needed to really evaluate our relationship."

Both of them looked at her as if they were trying to figure out what in the world she was thinking.

"Well, I can tell you that of all of my brothers, it's Jonah who's always known exactly what he wants out of life. Jonah doesn't do anything he doesn't want to do. Yes, he's a great guy and he will do anything for anybody. But he doesn't do it because he has to; he does it because he wants to. And when he wants something, he goes after it with everything in him. That's why he's built this amazing business; people from all over trust him with their hugely expensive yachts and boats. He's done so well for himself and it's strictly been because he wanted it and he went for it. I can tell you he's not telling you anything that he doesn't want to tell you or to do. Yes, he might be sympathetic to you and if he loves you, which is what I believe, then he's not doing it out of sympathy—it's out of love."

Her heart thundered, rolling downhill and gaining momentum; it was going to crash off a cliff if she wasn't careful. "That's kind of the same thing he said, but in different words. But how can I trust that? How can I know sometime down the line he won't regret not having his own children?"

Rosie took both of her hands in hers. "Are you listening to what you're saying? You are perfect for him, and I haven't known him anywhere near as long as Erin has known him. I know that the man, when he gets his mind set on something, he goes for it. And he will be a wonderful father. I don't care if your children are adopted or are your biological children—they are still your children. And when you're speaking that negativity, it's almost as if you don't believe that's true."

"Oh, no, I'm thrilled and excited to have this opportunity. I wanted to carry a child of my own in my womb but I will be grateful and will be blessed to choose some children to adopt and give a home to and love them with all my heart."

"Then why can't you think that Jonah, our tender-hearted giant, couldn't do the same thing? That man has so much love to give. And you're sitting there, denying him that. Now, if you don't love him, I totally get it. But if you love him, I'm very baffled." Rosie crossed her arms and her pretty eyes stared holes through Summer.

Was she really this person who couldn't think loving an adopted child was truly a blessing? It hit her hard and made her feel terrible. It was basically the same thing Hunter had said.

Erin wrapped her hands around her coffee mug and studied the dark contents. And then she lifted her gaze to Summer's. "I think that that's not who you are. I think that you're just a woman in a very hard situation. You still have so many issues to deal with and I can see where you would be worried that a man like Jonah would want to protect you and say something like that because he didn't want to hurt you. But that's not Jonah. So I'm going to urge you to get over that. Tell Jonah you need to take it slow, if you love him. If you don't love him, then I would cut it off.

"But if you love him, believe me—that man has been so ready for a wife. He's had plenty of opportunities, plenty of female companionship, so it's not like he's desperate. He sees, just like he always has all of his life, what he wants and there is nothing you can say to him that's going to change his mind. So you'll just have to believe him and move forward, or break his heart and move on. But he can help you heal and he wants to. Anyway, that's between you and him. Sounds to me like the best friend advice that I can offer you is that you and my brother need to talk some more."

"Yes, I think you're right." And she did think she was right. She just had to be ready for the conversation.

* * *

Jonah was working on getting barnacles off one of the boats, needing physical exertion like he had been needing ever since he had last spoke with Summer. It had been a week and he had forced himself to stay away. It had been one of the hardest things that he had done in his life but he had taken Tate's advice. His brother was long gone now, having flown out two days ago to somewhere to climb a mountain. And his brother—probably the least domestic fella of all of his brothers—had always been that way and he gave good advice. Sometimes the world just did not make sense. Tate Sinclair: macho man, adventurer extraordinaire, and he gave good relationship advice. Who knew?

But the more Jonah had thought about what Tate had said, the more he knew he needed to give Summer space. He needed to just be there in the background and be ready to help her in any way he could. But he did not need to put any kind of pressure on her. And he wasn't going to.

The sun was beating down on him as he scraped

the barnacles from the hull of the boat. It was a gorgeous older sailboat that was worth who knew how much money. It had been restored and used; it wasn't just sitting in some amazing boathouse on view for a few friends of the wealthy guy who owned it. No, it was put to great fun in the water but it was taken care of.

"That looks like really hot work."

He dropped the scraper as he spun to find Summer standing on the upper dock, smiling at him. "Summer, what are you doing here?"

She looked hesitant. "Hoping to find you with time to talk."

"I always have time to talk to you." He picked up a rag and wiped his hands off and then grabbed his shirt off the rail from where it hung off the pier. He quickly put it on and then looked at her. "I'm glad you're here."

"I'm glad that you're glad. I wasn't sure if you would welcome me again."

"Now, you know that's not true. I'll welcome you any time."

"That's what I hoped. Can we take a walk? Maybe get some ice cream?"

"Sure. I can always eat ice cream."

She chuckled. "That's what you said before."

They walked down the dock and got on the main boardwalk. They walked toward the big long pier where all the tourists and all the locals went to fish off of and where their favorite ice cream shop was. When they got there, she ordered strawberry and he ordered vanilla coconut. They walked over to stand near the railing.

After they had both taken a few bites of their ice cream, she faced him. "I was wrong, Jonah. I was scared. And I have opened up and told people about my past, including your sister and sister-in-law. So I'm taking the pressure off you—you're not the only person who knows my troubling history. But I'm nervous. I wanted to take back what I said. Jonah, I love you. And you said the most beautiful words to me a few days ago and I rejected them. But I haven't forgotten them. I think about them every day. And Erin and Rosie told me that I was missing out on basically the best thing that could happen to me if I talked myself into believing that you didn't know what you wanted. So I'm here with my heart open wide and all my insecurities and troubles and worries set aside. I'm here to ask you one question."

He reached behind him and dropped his ice cream cone into the trash can. And then gave her his full attention. "I am all ears. What question do you have to ask me?"

She handed him her ice cream. "Can you get rid of that for me, too? I don't need it melting all over me."

He took the ice cream cone and dropped it into the trash too, and then he took her hands. "You're trembling. What do you need to ask me that makes you shake?"

"I'm here to ask you if you love me."

"If that's the question you need to ask me, then you already have my answer. Yes, I love you. Yes, I want to stand by you. Yes, I want to live the rest of my life with you. Nothing else matters. And nothing has changed. Nothing will ever change that. I'm just going to sit back here and be patient and wait for you—at least hope that you didn't find somebody else while I was waiting."

"Never. I could never find anyone more suited to me or more loved by me than you."

His face transformed as relief washed off him. He embraced her and kissed her gently. "You scared me, I'm not going to lie."

She studied him. "Me too. I'm a work in progress but I'm starting to find my way."

"And I'm going to walk beside you the rest of the way."

"So I get to ask you a question."

She squeezed his hands with hers. "I hope it's the question that I want you to ask me."

He laughed and went down on one knee. "Summer, will you marry me? In your time, when it's right for you and no sooner. I just want to know if, at the end of all that, you're going to be mine."

She wrapped her arms around his neck, sank down onto his knee, and stared into his beautiful, beautiful eyes. "Jonah Sinclair, I never thought you were going to ask me to marry you." She grinned at the ridiculousness of teasing him at a moment like this. "Yes, I'll marry you. And I can't wait."

EPILOGUE

Two weeks later, Jonah and Summer walked out of the courthouse in Houston, hand in hand. All of his brothers walked in front of them as a barrier and Hunter and her father walked behind Summer. All of the Sinclair women, except his mother who stayed with Summer's mother to watch Polly, followed them. They had all come to support Summer as she faced her assailant. She was very strong and said what she had to say when it was her time, and then she had walked out of there with her entourage. And now she felt as if she were walking into her future. She still had a ways to go but her nightmares were getting better and she and Jonah were starting to plan a future together. She had a lot to look forward to and the last thing she was going to do was let her past rule her future.

And with Jonah and her friends, she was going to get through this. Her future sparkled with hope and promise.

When they finally walked from the courthouse, Jonah had his arm around her and everyone trailed behind them surrounding her with support as the TV cameras swarmed them. She answered a few questions but as the questions grew intrusive and the camera crews grew more aggressive she was swept through the throng by the Sinclair men and Hunter making a way for them while Jonah shielded her with his body. When they reached the waiting SUV with Jonah's dad waiting behind the wheel they climbed inside and Jonah pulled the door shut as cameras flashed.

"I hear you did good, sweetheart," Leo Sinclair said over his shoulder as he pressed the gas pedal and slowly drove them through the crowd. He had opted to be the drive-away car and someone must have called him about her statement to the attacker because that wasn't televised.

"She did amazing," Jonah said, still holding her close with his arm. "How are you now?"

She trembled, it had all been overwhelming but with so much support she'd made it. "I'm good. Very good. Now, it's in my past."

Jonah kissed her temple. "Yes, it is. You were my hero in there today, Summer. You were amazing, and stood up for yourself. You got your power back."

Her heart felt full. "I did. But you and everyone from Sunset Bay gave me strength. I hope everyone knows how much I valued them being there and the kind support from those who couldn't make the trip."

"They know, but if you are up for it we are going to celebrate with everyone when we get home. But only if you are up to it."

Her heart felt fuller than before, as if it would burst with happiness. "I'm so ready to celebrate,"

"Then I'll let them know we're showing up. I love you, Summer."

"And I love you. I'm so glad we were brought

together." She watched his eyes light up just the way she loved to see them.

"Me too. I've been waiting on you all of my life and it was worth the wait."

She sighed, placed her head on his shoulder. "For me too."

* * *

Tate watched as the SUV carrying Jonah and Summer pulled away from the curb. The look of complete love on his brother's face hit it a chord inside him and standing there now, he knew that the restlessness he'd been feeling lately was him wanting more. More of what his brothers and his sister, Erin, had found. He'd never felt that way before. But maybe being open to the idea was the first step.

His phone rang and he answered it when he saw it was his agent.

"Tate, I hate to bother you, I know you wanted time off, but Greg Arron has been injured. He's in the hospital, he's banged up pretty bad but going to recover. But they need you on the set to replace him. I told them you'd make time for this. If not for your own career I figure you'd do it to help Greg out."

Greg Arron had been one of the men who had given him his start as a stuntman. It had been a natural way to use his sense of adventure and make a living that could help him fuel his adventures. And this was a super A-list blockbuster. He'd wanted time off but that would have to wait until after he helped Greg out by keeping his company in the picture. "Send me the ticket and I'll be there tonight."

"That's what I thought. It's already on its way to your inbox."

"Send me Greg's info, I need to call him and drop by on my way in."

"Will do."

He hung up and went to tell his brothers. His personal life would have to wait, just a little longer. What he did for a living had its risks. Greg was an example of a man who followed the rules, was the best of the best and still, there was a margin for error. Serious error.

Was he ready to give it up, or bring a future family into his risky lifestyle?

He had a lot to think about. And yet, as he caught a plane a couple of hours later he kept seeing Jonah's content and happy expression in is mind's eye.

And as he looked out over the clouds he suddenly felt lonelier than he'd ever felt in his life...

More Books by Debra Clopton

Turner Creek Ranch Series
Treasure Me, Cowboy (Book 1)
Rescue Me, Cowboy (Book 2)
Complete Me, Cowboy (Book 3)
Sweet Talk Me, Cowboy (Book 4)

Texas Matchmaker Series
Dream With Me, Cowboy (Book 1)
Be My Love, Cowboy (Book 2)
This Heart's Yours, Cowboy (Book 3)
Hold Me, Cowboy (Book 4)
Be Mine, Cowboy (Book 5)
Marry Me, Cowboy (Book 6)
Cherish Me, Cowboy (Book 7)
Surprise Me, Cowboy (Book 8)
Serenade Me, Cowboy (Book 9)
Return To Me, Cowboy (Book 10)
Love Me, Cowboy (Book 11)
Ride With Me, Cowboy (Book 12)
Dance With Me, Cowboy (Book 13)

Windswept Bay Series
From This Moment On (Book 1)
Somewhere With You (Book 2)
With This Kiss (Book 3)
Forever and For Always (Book 4)
Holding Out For Love (Book 5)
With This Ring (Book 6)
With This Promise (Book 7)
With This Pledge (Book 8)
With This Wish (Book 9)
With This Forever (Book 10)
With This Vow (Book 11)

About the Author

Bestselling author Debra Clopton has sold over 2.5 million books. Her book OPERATION: MARRIED BY CHRISTMAS has been optioned for an ABC Family Movie. Debra is known for her contemporary, western romances, Texas cowboys and feisty heroines. Sweet romance and humor are always intertwined to make readers smile. A sixth generation Texan she lives with her husband on a ranch deep in the heart of Texas. She loves being contacted by readers.

Visit Debra's website at www.debraclopton.com

Sign up for Debra's newsletter at www.debraclopton.com/contest/

Check out her Facebook at www.facebook.com/debra.clopton.5

Follow her on Twitter at @debraclopton

Contact her at debraclopton@ymail.com

If you enjoyed reading *Longing for Ever After* I would appreciate it if you would help others enjoy this book, too.

Recommend it. Please help other readers find this book by recommending it to friends, reader's groups and discussion boards.

Review it. Please tell other readers why you liked this book by reviewing it on the retail site you purchased it from or Goodreads. If you do write a review, please send an email to debraclopton@ymail.com so I can thank you with a personal email. Or visit me at: www.debraclopton.com.